"Maybe you sh[ould] to me," Jake said quietly.

At those words, Cat's world flipped over. At first she thought he wasn't going to meet her eyes, but then he looked at her squarely and she saw the tumult of emotions in them. For a wild moment, she wondered if maybe she and Jake had a chance to go back in time and be together again.

"I wouldn't try to push myself into your lives. I promise," he said after a moment. "I just—well, if you were closer I wouldn't worry about the two of you so much."

"Oh." Cat felt all of her wild imaginings fall back to earth with a thud. She had somehow forgotten how responsible Jake felt for everything and everyone. Of course, he would want to do his duty by her and Lara. She just knew that love was a far cry from duty, and she had searched for love her whole life.

She needed to remember she had come here for Lara. Her own feelings didn't matter.

She looked down at her daughter. Cat needed to be strong for her.

Books by Janet Tronstad

JANET TRONSTAD

grew up on a family farm in Montana where, like the Stone brothers in this book, she had a bedroom window that, if left open on certain spring nights, would bring the fragrance of lilacs into the room. She used those memories in writing this book. Janet lives in Pasadena, California now, but often spends time back on her family's farm in Montana. She has written almost thirty books, many of them in the Dry Creek series.

Lilac Wedding in Dry Creek

Janet Tronstad

Love Inspired

Recycling programs
for this product may
not exist in your area.

™ LOVE INSPIRED BOOKS

ISBN-13: 978-0-373-87727-0

LILAC WEDDING IN DRY CREEK

Copyright © 2012 by Janet Tronstad

www.LoveInspiredBooks.com

Printed in U.S.A.

If thou canst believe,
all things are possible to him that believeth.
—*Mark* 9:23

This book is dedicated to my friend, David White,
with love and affection.

Chapter One

Distant thunder rumbled as Jake Stone lifted his duffel bag onto his shoulder, closed his door and started walking down the hall toward the lobby of the Starling Hotel. It was a rainy day in March and he didn't look forward to the long drive north to Dry Creek, Montana—especially because once he got there his older brother would start pressing him even harder to move back to the ranch, settle down and get married.

Jake refused to marry some poor woman just to stop his brother from nagging him to death. The Stone boys had bad history when it came to family life, even if his brother chose to ignore it. As for moving back to Dry Creek, Jake had decided years ago that this nondescript hotel near the Las Vegas airport was home enough for him.

He entered the lobby and glanced over to where the owner of the place stood behind the counter.

"Well, don't you look fine?" Gray stubble showed on Max Holden's weathered face, but his eyes were lively as he looked up. "Going home to Dry Creek for your brother's wedding is doing you good already."

Jake stopped and ran a finger around the collar of his new white shirt so he could breathe easier.

"Got some stamps?" He finished walking over to the counter, dropped his duffel bag to the floor and reached into the back pocket of his jeans, pulling out an envelope and handing it to the other man.

Jake didn't like to talk about the wedding. His brother was wrong if he thought getting married would change who he was in the eyes of their small hometown. Not that Jake blamed anyone for how they felt about the Stone family. Everyone knew about the years of physical abuse out at their ranch. All of the family secrets had been laid bare when his father was murdered and his mother had gone to trial for doing the crime. People naturally had wondered if the sons were more like their father or their mother. Neither answer had been good back then.

Max took the long, white envelope from Jake and weighed it in his hand. "I figure two stamps should do it." Then he glanced down at the writing on the front. "I hope this Cathy Barker appreciates all the letters you send. Who is she, anyway?"

So much time had passed since Jake heard someone speak the woman's name that he hadn't expected the jolt that went through him. Max had never questioned the envelopes before.

Secrets had destroyed Jake's family as surely as his father's alcoholism. If his mother had confided in their neighbors, then they might have understood what was happening. And she might not have served a ten-year prison term before anyone realized she was innocent and had only confessed to protect her teenage sons from facing suspicion.

"We used to call her Cat," Jake began and forced himself to set forth the whole story. "I don't know how she feels or even if she gets the letters. I put my return address on every one, but she never writes back."

At that bit of information, Max's jaw dropped along with the envelope.

"You mean to tell me, all these years you've been stuffing those letters with cash—and don't think I don't know what's in there—then asking me to mail them like they were your last will and testament. And you don't even know whether or not they're getting through to her."

Rain continued to pound against the windows as Jake tried to think of an answer that didn't make him seem like a half wit. Nothing came to mind. It sounded foolish to admit that it eased his worries to send her money.

"You're sure about sending this?" Max asked as he looked down at the envelope now resting on his counter. "What if you have another dry spell? You might not always be winning at the poker tables like you have been. And, there's a lot of money in there."

Jake glanced over his shoulder. The lobby was empty. But, through the main windows, he could see the figure of a woman walking down the street toward the motel, trying to hold a black umbrella open in front of her against the wind. As near as he could tell, it looked as if she was rolling a big suitcase behind her. He had only a few minutes before she got here.

Jake turned back to Max. He'd have to talk fast. "If

I keep my expenses like they are now, I have enough money in the bank to last me a hundred and fifteen years. I don't plan on living nearly that long, and Cat might need something today. She's a friend from the youth home—you know, the place where they sent me and my youngest brother when they shipped my mother off to prison and my older brother joined the rodeo circuit. No one there will ever give me Cat's address, but they always promise to forward the letters for me."

Jake had never strung so many words together in his life and he was starting to regret it.

Max cleared his throat and nodded. "I know how it is. There are guys from Vietnam I'd send my last dollar to if they needed it. You go through something like that with someone, you never forget them."

Jake nodded. Maybe it wasn't so bad to bare his soul after all.

Then the door clicked open behind him and the wind blew cold air inside, making the back of his neck shiver. He didn't turn to see who was there. The anxious frown on Max's face was enough to scare the woman away without him adding to it. Thinking of Cat always unnerved him.

"Mommy?" The voice of a young girl sounded uncertain behind him.

He'd been mistaken in thinking it was a suitcase beside the woman, Jake realized. He was usually more observant, but the rain on the windows had made it difficult to see. Still, he didn't turn around. He figured a woman with any sense would be shepherding her little one out of the Starling about now. One good look at the run-down hotel would be all it would take to give a mother with a young child second thoughts about staying there. The place had heart, but the color from the linoleum had faded away to nothing over the years. He should give Max some money to replace the linoleum with carpet. Jake had the money to give and Max had been good to him over the years.

"Can I help you?" Max finally asked as he looked past Jake. He must have expected the woman to be gone by now, too. "Our business is mostly by the month. There's a nice family motel around the corner and down a block, though. It's a little more expensive, but they've got a small pool. Ask for the spring special and they'll treat you right."

"I am looking for 3762 Morgan Street," the woman said. "I think it must be a house or an apartment. I didn't see any numbers outside your place and I wondered if you'd know how close I am."

Jake lost all feeling in his body before she got to the street name. He knew that voice as well as he knew his own.

"You got a package or something?" Max asked, suddenly cautious.

"I'm looking for a man. Jake Stone. He lives there."

Max gave a start and his bulging eyes went to Jake as if he was waiting for some signal as to what he should say to the woman.

Jake would have been happy to oblige, but something had happened in his brain and everything was going in slow motion. It sounded as though the woman's words were coming from a great distance. He needed to sit down, but he couldn't move. His boots kept him rooted to the place where he stood.

"My name's Cat—I mean, Cathy Barker. If you know where I could find the address, I'd appreciate it very much if you'd point me in the right direction. I had planned to take a taxi from the airport, but none of them had a child's safety seat so I just left our luggage in the claim section and we started to walk. They said it wasn't far when they told me how to find the street."

Max's face turned a little purple at her flow of words.

"You're…" He started to sputter and then stopped. Finally, he pointed. "That's him. This is the address right here."

Everything was silent for a moment.

"Jake?"

The hesitation in the woman's voice brought Jake to his senses. He didn't want to stand with his back to her like a fake statue, not when Cat might just be passing through and only wanted to say hello. He bluffed at the poker tables in one casino or another almost every night. He should be able to school his face into some semblance of normalcy and turn around and greet his old friend.

"Mommy, is that him?" the girl asked.

Jake felt his breath catch in his throat. He forced his lips to stretch into a smile as he turned around.

There she was. Cat. She hadn't changed a bit, he thought, as she stared up at him, her green eyes growing large and her delicate face turning pale. Her chin still jutted out as if she expected a fight, but her golden-brown hair had been blown around enough to show she didn't even have the strength to battle the wind on her own. And that was before the rain had plastered every strand of hair to the side of her head. He'd always protected her and he felt like doing it now.

"I…" Cat started to say something, but stopped.

"Mommy?" The small voice grew more incessant and worried. Jake glanced down and saw that the girl had a plastic, gold tiara clamped onto her damp blond hair. She wasn't much taller than the stool behind Max's counter and her pink cheeks made her look like a cherub in some old European painting. She had gold glitter sticking on her shoes, too, in spite of the rain. Jake was going to say something to soothe her, but then she reached for her mother's hand.

He looked up in time to see Cat's eyes start to close. If he hadn't stepped over to catch her, she would have drifted all the way to the floor. As it was, she didn't weigh more than a feather when he lifted her in his arms. He wanted to ask when the last time was that she'd eaten a decent meal. He hadn't seen her for five years and she certainly hadn't gained an ounce in all that time. He wondered what she had spent all of the money he mailed her on. It certainly hadn't been food, not when she'd just fainted the way she had.

Jake caught the subtle scent of lilacs as he looked down. He'd presented Cat with a whole case of lilac soap for her eighteenth birthday.

"Mommy?" the girl said again, but this time the word had an edge to it, as though she was frightened.

Cat's little girl stared up at him, expecting something.

"It'll be all right," he assured her. "Your mother just needs to eat something."

He remembered Cat had fainted a time or two when

she first came to the youth home. The nurse said it was because she hadn't eaten then, too.

The child nodded. Her curls were starting to bounce, but her blue eyes still watched him closely. It seemed she didn't quite trust him, even if she wasn't withdrawing from him. She reached up to steady her tiara, not saying anything.

He stepped past the girl and carried Cat over to the sofa. He laid her down on the vinyl sofa, arranging her head so it rested on one sofa arm while her feet curved up on the other one. The upholstery creaked softly as it adjusted to her being there.

Cat had run away from the youth home the day after he gave her the lilac soap, taking every one of the bars with her. She must be almost twenty-three now. She was only a few months younger than him.

He reached for her face, hoping to bring her back. "Cat?"

Her skin was wet and cold from being outside, but he felt his fingers tingle where they touched her. He took his Stetson off and set it on the back of the sofa. Then he leaned down and kissed her on the forehead. It wasn't proper, but he couldn't help himself. This was Cat.

"Are you a prince?" Suddenly the girl was beside him. She sounded suspicious and she moved even closer, as though she wanted to be sure she could see everything he did.

Jake leaned back and looked over at her in surprise. "A what?"

He'd been called many things in his life, but never that.

The girl's tiara was crooked by now, but she didn't

seem to notice. "In *Sleeping Beauty,* the prince kisses the princess and she wakes up."

"I don't think…"

The girl's eyes narrowed. "Maybe you're not doing it right. Kiss her again so her eyes open."

Jake looked back down at Cat. Her daughter had a point. The first kiss certainly hadn't moved any mountains.

"On the lips," the girl instructed him as he started toward her mother's forehead. "It has to be on the lips for it to work. It says so in my book."

Who was he to argue with an expert? Especially one who had a book to back her up.

Cat felt Jake's lips brush hers, but she couldn't rouse herself enough to respond. She'd had that dream so many times, and it never turned out to be real. Only, now her heart was racing and she felt the chill of the vinyl sofa under her and the gentleness of his hand when he caressed her cheek. Everything else was a kaleidoscope of colors, but maybe it wasn't just her imagination this time. She'd taken her heart medication this morning, hadn't she? She tried to remember and the moment started to come back. She'd flown from Minneapolis with her daughter, Lara, because time had become so important and the bus would have taken too long.

Had she heard Lara talking about a prince? The first thing Lara had packed in her suitcase was the book of fairy tales she'd received at Christmas. She loved those stories. It was the thought of her daughter that made Cat fight all the way back to awareness. Everything she did these days had to be about Lara.

Jake's hand rested against her face. She hated to move because he might take his hand away. But she willed her eyes to open. She saw Jake frowning down on her, his black eyes almost setting off sparks, he was looking at her so intently. She blinked and he came into focus. Yes, he was even more handsome—and fierce— than she recalled.

No wonder Lara thought he was a prince. His thick black hair was styled back, longer than she remembered it. And far more sophisticated than it had been at the youth home. He'd spent some money on having it cut. His face had been thinner back then, too. Now it was filled out with all the muscles and power of a man in his prime. He still had what he called his "Cherokee nose," inherited from his Native American grandfather. Jake wasn't the lanky teenager who'd been her gallant defender in the home, but she would have recognized him anywhere. His eyes gave him away. No one looked at her like Jake did. He saw inside of her.

She wondered for the first time if she would have come here even without Lara. She was suddenly glad to see him just in case the heart surgery didn't go well. He'd been the best friend she'd ever had and she wanted to remember his face forever.

"Could I have something to drink?" she whispered.

Then she closed her eyes. She didn't fear the possibility of death, but she did fear what would happen to Lara without her. Before she left Minneapolis, she'd had a conversation with the chaplain at the hospital where she hoped to have her surgery. The man had led her back to the God she'd known briefly as a young girl.

Her faith helped her accept what was happening. Her heart was defective and had been since she was born. It's just that now it was critical that something be done. The doctors wanted to do surgery right away, even though she might not survive it. Finally, she told them all that everything would need to wait until she got her daughter settled.

She opened her eyes and saw a new face looking down at her. The older man from the counter was now standing next to Jake.

"I have coffee right here," he said as he handed a cup to Jake. "I can get her something stronger than coffee if I need to. But it's supposed to wake people up so I figure…"

Cat wasn't used to strangers worrying about her and she wanted to tell the older man that she appreciated his concern, but it was too much effort.

"Just water," she managed to say. She should take one of the heart pills the doctor had given her, if she could find a way to take it without alarming either of the men. She wasn't ready to tell Jake everything yet. Let him get to know Lara a little first. She had to believe that, if he spent enough time with her daughter, he would be willing to take care of her if needed. She had no one else to ask and she couldn't let Lara go into the foster-care system. Jake would understand that.

"I'll be right back." The older man rushed away to get her what she needed.

Cat felt Lara's hand on her arm and looked over to see that her daughter had squeezed in front of where

Jake was kneeling. Everything about her was pale next to the blackness of his hair and the light brown color of his forehead, but they looked good together. As though they belonged. Cat put her own hand over her daughter's.

"I'm fine, pumpkin." The words were hard to form, but she kept working at it. "I just need to catch my breath."

Lara smiled, her blue eyes dancing in quiet delight.

"He kissed you," she whispered, a little too loud to be private. "I saw everything, and then you woke up. Just like in *Sleeping Beauty*."

"Ahhh," Cat murmured as she reached out and touched her daughter's cheek. "Maybe it's not quite the same. *Sleeping Beauty* is a story."

She had no strength to continue. They'd already had this discussion, anyway. Lara insisted on believing her fairy tales were real no matter what Cat said.

"I'm going to call an ambulance," Jake suddenly said as he reached toward his pocket—probably for a cell phone. "In case this isn't just hunger."

He was looking at her with a dozen questions in his eyes. None of which she wanted to answer.

"I'll be fine," Cat repeated, this time looking away from her daughter and facing him squarely. She willed him to believe her.

"You can be fine in an ambulance, too," he said as he held his cell phone and started to dial.

She shook her head. Then she reached out a hand and motioned for him to move over slightly and draw closer so she could whisper and only he would hear. "I just need to rest a minute. And I don't want to scare Lara."

She didn't need a doctor to tell her what she already knew.

"She's not worried," Jake murmured, and then his lips actually curved up slightly. "She thinks I'm her private prince, here to do her bidding, anyway. Like some genie in a bottle."

Cat smiled. She put her hand on his shoulder and felt the dampness of his shirt. "I got you all wet."

She could also feel the warmth of his skin through the shirt.

"It's okay."

She noticed then that his face was damp, too. She must have flung rain drops everywhere. Odd that his hair was dry. His eyes were searching hers. He always did take his responsibilities to heart. Poor Jake. She wondered if he'd rescued any more damsels in distress after she'd left the home. She had meant to spare him that.

He leaned down farther until he was almost near enough to kiss her again. Her mouth felt suddenly dry and she wished so many things were different in her life. She hadn't been a particularly good damsel for him to rescue years ago, but now she was hopeless. She had far too many problems for any white knight to solve. And this one deserved better.

Just then the other man came back with a bottle of water, and Jake pulled away.

"I have a refrigerator in the storeroom so I can keep things cold," the man said, not seeming to notice the tension in the air. "I have a microwave, too, if you'd rather have hot water."

"Maybe later," she said. "I have some crackers in my purse and I could…"

She saw Jake scowl and start to rise.

"Cold water is perfect now, though." Cat braced her arms so she could push herself up into a sitting position on the couch. Then she reached for the water. "That's just what I need."

"What you need is a big steak and a baked potato," Jake muttered. By now he was standing and glowering down at her. "When did you eat last? And I don't mean crackers."

She had forgotten how it was with Jake. He liked to rescue damsels, but he was opinionated as he did it. She didn't have energy to challenge him now, though. "I had something on the airplane coming out here."

"Pretzels, I suppose. They're not any better."

Cat leaned her head back and took a drink. At least Jake believed it was hunger that had made her faint. That would satisfy him for a while. Give her time to think. She hadn't quite expected the surge of tenderness that struck her when he was so close. She hoped it wouldn't make it more difficult to ask him what she needed to when the time came.

"You're here on a stopover then?" He hesitated. For a moment he looked vulnerable. "How long do you have?"

"As much time as you have to spare."

The tension left his eyes. "Well, when you finish with that water, I'm going to see about getting you something to eat, then. I'm surprised that wind didn't blow you away out there."

"I don't want to be any trouble." Even as she said it,

she knew it was too late for her to be anything but that. She just hoped she didn't disrupt his life too much.

"What does Lara like to eat?" he asked, turning to leave but not yet stepping away.

"She eats almost anything except peas." Cat was glad the conversation wasn't about her anymore.

There was a rustle at her side, and she saw her daughter wiggle in between them again, now that Jake was standing.

"Peas are ugly," her daughter announced, looking up at Jake defiantly. When he didn't say anything, she started to talk faster. "And, I'm a princess, so if I get peas under my mattress, I won't be able to sleep all night long. And, they make me burp." She paused and looked down at the floor. "Well, sort of—sometimes."

Cat had struggled to teach Lara the difference between truth and lies, even before she got the book of fairy tales. At first, Cat thought the book was good because it helped Lara learn to read, but she was beginning to wonder if Lara really believed she was a princess when she said things like that.

"Don't worry. I'll get you carrots," Jake said as he squatted down to her daughter's level. His voice was gentle and he seemed to really be looking at her. "I'm not that fond of peas, either."

Lara beamed at him.

Jake just looked at the girl for another minute.

"How old are you, Lara?" he finally asked.

Cat felt her breath clutch. She suddenly realized he was asking the question as if he didn't know the answer. She'd taken for granted that he'd known that much. She wasn't ready to tell him everything, but he must know who Lara was. She hadn't even worried about that on the way here.

"I'm four," her daughter answered, and held up the required number of fingers with the confidence of her preschool training. "And three months."

Cat saw the shock wave go through Jake and she reached her hand out to stop him from saying a word. She hadn't told her daughter anything, but surely Jake had known.

"Lara, will you take the bottle back to the nice man at the counter?" she asked as she held the plastic water bottle out to her daughter.

Fortunately, Jake knew what she intended and waited to say anything until Lara had walked over to the older man and he lifted her up on a stool.

"Who's her father?" Jake's voice was low and impatient.

Cat took a quick breath. "I thought you knew. It's you."

"Me?" Jake turned to stare at her fully. She couldn't read his face. He'd gone pale. That much she could see. And his jaw was tense.

She nodded and darted a look over at Lara. "I know she doesn't look like you, but I promise I wasn't with anyone else. Not after we…"

She didn't even have any proof, she realized. She hadn't thought she would ever need any. She hadn't put his name on the birth certificate, either.

"Of course you weren't with anyone else," Jake said indignantly. "We were so tight there would have been no time to…" He stopped and lifted his hand to rub the back of his neck. "At least, I thought we were tight. Until you ran away."

His voice had drifted, but it was still loud enough to be overheard and she lifted her hand to ask him to lower it. But then he went completely silent, just crouched there looking at her. Soon his black eyes warmed until they were filled with golden flecks. She'd forgotten they could do that.

"She's really mine?" he whispered, his voice husky once again.

Cat nodded. "She doesn't know. Although she doesn't take after you—her hair and everything—she's got your way of looking out at the world. I assumed someone on the staff at the youth home must have told you about her…"

His jaw tensed further at that.

"You think I wouldn't have moved heaven and earth to find you if I'd known you'd had my baby?" Jake's eyes flashed. He'd obviously forgotten about being quiet. "I made several trips back to the home to try and trace you. They said you didn't want to be found so I finally accepted that. But if I'd known I had a daughter, I would have forced them to tell me where you were. I'd have gotten some high-powered lawyer and made them talk."

Cat suddenly realized why she'd been so sure he knew. "But you've been sending me money. No letters. Just the money. Why would you do that? I thought it was like child support in your mind. That you wanted to be responsible even if you didn't want to be involved with us."

Jake shook his head. "I didn't put down any words

because I didn't know what to say. I thought the money spoke for itself. That you would write when you were ready. And the money—it was like a tithe."

"A tithe? You're going to church?" Cat asked in relief. Maybe God had worked things out better than she had hoped. If Jake was a Christian, then she would feel so much better about him raising Lara if it came to that.

He shook his head. "Churches never have been any use to me, you know that. But I remember something Mrs. Hargrove gave me when I was a kid. You remember the lady who used to write me when I was in the home?" He looked at Cat until she nodded. "Well, one of the church papers talked about tithing."

Cat was confused. "People give tithes to *churches.*"

Jake nodded. "Yes, so the church can help those in need. I am just cutting out the middle man. I figured you could use food and things so I gave the money to you."

"Charity?" she whispered, appalled. She'd never imagined that was what the envelopes of cash were about.

Jake lowered his eyes, but he didn't deny anything.

"I had money. Not much, but I didn't need charity," she finally managed to say before she heard Lara squeal and come running back to the sofa.

Cat willed her heart to stay steady. She couldn't afford to get upset. She breathed as deeply as she dared and stayed silent. Jake's eyes were caught by Lara, anyway.

"Come here, princess," he said softly to the girl as

she danced closer. The ballet shoes had been a present last Christmas, too. "Let me look at you."

Lara twirled around and faced him, her cheeks flushed with merriment. "Are you going to turn me into a toad?"

Jake grinned. "Not today."

Her daughter was enchanting, Cat thought in relief. No one could resist her.

Jake did seem interested in Lara, but that wouldn't be enough, Cat reminded herself. She hadn't even asked the crucial question yet. Now she wasn't so sure. Jake had always been the first one to stand up and do what was right. But that didn't equal love. She knew that better than anyone and she didn't want Lara to grow up feeling as though she was a burden on someone.

Cat reminded herself that's why she had run away from Jake and the home all those years ago. She'd known back then that he'd marry her for duty, but it wasn't enough. What if Jake agreed to take Lara, but then treated her like a charity child? He might as well turn her into a toad right now and be done with it.

What had possessed him to send her all that money, anyway? She'd just assumed he knew she'd had a baby seven months after she left the home and had done the math. Over the years, he had sent her forty or fifty thousand dollars. She worked as a waitress at first, and some months she wouldn't have made rent without his help. Even now that she worked in an office, she didn't really make enough to do without his assistance. At least she had medical insurance, she told herself.

But money wasn't everything. She wanted more than that for Lara.

Dear Lord, she thought finally. *I need Your help here. Lara needs a father and not an imaginary prince who will break her heart. And I need wisdom to know if he is the right one to raise her if I can't. He might be her biological father, but will he come to love her as a father should? Every little girl needs to be loved, whether she's a princess or not.*

Chapter Two

Jake pulled out his cell phone when he got back to the counter. Max was looking at him with concern in his eyes, but Jake wasn't ready to talk about anything yet. His whole life had been picked up and spun around in a whirlwind before landing him back in the same place. He found he couldn't remember the number to any restaurant in town.

He finally gave up and looked at his old friend. "I'm a father."

"What?" Max frowned and leaned closer as though he hadn't heard the words right.

"A father. You know—man, woman, baby."

Max stared at him. "What are you talking about?"

Jake looked toward Lara. The girl was sitting on the sofa by her mother and adjusting her tiara again. Suddenly, she giggled at something Cat had said.

"But she's blonde with blue eyes!" Max had followed Jake's gaze and then turned back.

Jake nodded. Her hair wasn't just blond, it was naturally curly.

"And you're a quarter Cherokee with the black hair

to prove it. And your eyes are so brown they're almost black, in case you haven't looked in the mirror lately. Are you sure?" Then his face flushed. "You wouldn't be the first man to be fooled by a woman. Maybe Cat, maybe she—"

"No." Jake glared at his friend. "It was just Cat and me." His voice broke then. "I trust her with everything and especially that."

He tried to think of more words to explain and couldn't. "She's—Cat. She'd never lie to me."

They were both silent for a moment.

"You care about her, then?" Max asked gruffly. "This Cat of yours?"

The question surprised him. "Of course, we went through a lot together."

Even now, being torn between the misery of not having been told when Lara was born and the wonder of just learning that he had a daughter, he still knew Cat was some kind of an anchor in his life. Now that she was here, he didn't want her to leave. Max could probably see the feelings on his face. Not much escaped the old man.

Max's voice softened. "I don't suppose you asked her to marry you yet."

Jake snorted. "Of course I asked her—years ago. She ran away from the home the next day and I never saw her again. That's how well that went. Not that it was a good idea, anyway."

Max was silent as they both turned to look across the room to where Cat and Lara sat, curled up together on the sofa. The gray clouds were lifting and sunshine was streaming in through the large glass windows behind them.

"You probably didn't say it right," Max finally said. "You have a hard time getting to the point sometimes. I've noticed that."

"I said she should let me know if she got in trouble. I know a man's duty. I said I'd marry her if needed. It wasn't hard to misunderstand that. I didn't wrap it up in a bow, but she had to have heard me. She just didn't want to. Not that I blame her. I'm not any prize. You know about my father. None of the Stone men have any business setting up a family."

Max was quiet for another minute, also studying the mother and child. By now, the sunlight was shining on them directly.

Then Max looked back, and a grin split his face.

"That little girl? She's really yours?"

Jake nodded and started to grin, himself. "She doesn't know, so keep it quiet."

"That means I'm a grandpa!" Max whispered. He'd always said Jake was like a son to him. Then he reached over and flipped the switch on the counter that changed the sign outside to read No Vacancy. "Nobody needs to know why, but we have to do something. You're a father."

"I guess I am at that." Jake stood there, letting the amazement settle in deeper. Maybe it would be okay if he was a father as long as he wasn't close enough to the child to mess up her life. Cat had never said anything about telling Lara about him. Maybe the girl would never know.

Max frowned in thought. Then his face lit up. "We'll

have a birthday party. We've got lots of birthdays to make up for. Cake and ice cream. That should be okay."

"I sure feel like celebrating." Jake held the phone more firmly in his hand and started pressing buttons. He did know one number. "I'm calling that steakhouse in the new casino."

"The fancy one?" Max asked. "They don't even open until five o'clock. And they'll never deliver. Maybe they'd do room service in the casino, but not over here. And we need to get a cake. I wonder if the child has a favorite kind."

Jake put the phone to his ear. "They have that cake place there, too. I'm calling the head chef. He's always there at this time of day. And he's a good guy. Besides, he owes me. I handled a family problem for him a while back. His son was getting in with a bad crowd at the tables."

Max grinned again. "Get me some of those crab cakes, too, then."

With that, Max turned and opened the door behind the counter. Jake didn't have time to worry about what the older man was doing by disappearing into the storeroom, not when he had the best chef in Las Vegas on the line.

"How do you like your steaks?" Jake called over to Cat, putting down the phone to muffle the sound of his voice. "And how do you feel about mushrooms?"

The sight of Cat and Lara, sitting with their heads together, made something shift around inside him. He had a new purpose in life. Lara didn't need to know who he was for him to take care of her. He'd be some family friend that came to school plays once in a while.

He'd be the old man in the back of the church at her wedding and he'd give the presents with no name tag on them at holidays. He wouldn't even need to talk to her over the years. Just making sure she had enough to live a good life would be sufficient.

"Oh, don't order steaks," Cat said as she broke apart from her daughter and started to rise. "They're too expensive. I can walk over to that burger place around the corner. That'll be enough."

"Steak—well-done, medium or rare?" Jake asked again. "And stay seated. You're not walking anywhere. I don't want you fainting a second time. Especially not when the sidewalks are wet."

"I guess medium, if I have to choose." Cat sat back down and brushed her hair away from her face. "But really, it's not necessary. I never eat steak. And—"

"I'm paying," Jake interrupted, knowing what was troubling her. Before she came to the home all those years ago, she'd lived on the streets in Fargo.

Now that her hair was drying, it was starting to fly this way and that. Jake remembered the golden-brown halo around her face. She used to look like that when she was studying her math problems. She had that same indecisive look on her face, too. As if she wasn't sure of the right answer and didn't want to choose the wrong one.

"I guess it's all right, then," she said with a frown.

"And the mushrooms?" he asked.

"Canned or fresh?"

"Imported."

Now she looked bewildered. "I've never had an imported mushroom. What kind?"

"Porcini." Jake repeated what the chef had told him minutes before. "They also call them the black mushroom. Don't worry. They're good."

She looked at him in full amazement now. "You've *eaten* those mushrooms? You wouldn't even eat garlic at the home. Said it wasn't part of your culture. You, with your Cherokee-chief grandfather. You asked the cook to make you fry bread instead. Said the Cherokee were used to their own diet and they were in this country first and should be able to eat what they wanted. Then you used the table as a drum."

"I guess I was pretty difficult back then," he admitted.

"You were persuasive, too," Cat added as she bit her lip nervously. "The cook finally made it for you that one time. She said it was just to shut you up, but she made enough for everybody. It was like a party."

Trust Cat to find one of the few good memories related to that place.

Jake finished their order by adding roasted white corn with pepper, and truffle mashed potatoes. Then he checked with Lara and ordered a chocolate birthday cake with raspberry filling for dessert. He also asked for the crab cakes to please Max and some macaroni and cheese for Lara in case she didn't feel like eating what the rest of them did.

"Thirty minutes," Jake said when he hung up the phone. He'd never spent that kind of money for a meal before and he was surprised to discover it felt so good. He needed to do something to mark this day. He was a father. Maybe not a regular one with Little League and all, but it was more than he ever thought he'd be.

* * *

Cat brushed the hair away from her face as she sat down at the table. She couldn't believe it. Max and Jake had put a full box of purple candles on the chocolate cake sitting in the middle of the table. The men who brought the food had laid a white tablecloth over the folding table the older man had pulled out of the storeroom. The deliverymen had put real china plates down, too.

There was a big Happy Birthday banner taped to the counter and Jake had explained earlier to Lara that they were celebrating all of the birthdays he and Max had missed—all four of them together. For once Cat was glad for the fairy-tale book. Lara took the party in stride, as though that kind of thing happened every day for good little girls like her.

"They're fish," Lara said in delight from where she was seated. She was holding up some kind of macaroni on her fork and she was right; they were fish shaped.

"The chef thought of using one of our French cheeses," the thickset man who had laid out most of the food said. "But then he decided the little one might be more comfortable with some nice Wisconsin cheddar."

"Good choice," Cat said. All those years she'd been a waitress, she'd never seen anything like this. As for French cheeses—who had the money for that? "Thanks."

Right then, Jake stepped back into the lobby. He'd gone to his room to change out of his damp clothes. She and Lara didn't have their suitcases, but they had gone to a room and toweled themselves dry.

"Now, doesn't he look handsome?" Max winked at her from his chair as Jake got closer.

"I've never seen him in a suit." Cat feared she was blushing, but the older man was right. Jake was breathtaking in his dark suit and white shirt. He might have a whole closet full of clothes he wore in this new life of his. She looked closer. That suit was a tuxedo, even if the shirt was regular enough at first glance.

"That's his wedding suit," Max said proudly.

Cat felt her breath catch. Wedding! She'd never considered the possibility that Jake would be getting married. Or maybe was already married. If he was, that might change everything for Lara. Wicked stepmothers were the part of fairy tales that Cat believed, herself.

"Who is she?" Cat forced herself to ask. She'd try to keep an open mind.

"It's his brother," Max answered back.

She blinked at that, but before she could ask anything more, Jake stepped up to the table and sat in the remaining chair.

"What he's trying to say is that I'm going to be best man at my brother's wedding on Saturday so I'm trying the suit out," he said. "Making sure it's comfortable."

One of the men who had delivered the food placed the last glass on the table with a flourish. "That's everything."

Jake reached in his pocket and pulled out a handful of bills. "Thanks, everyone."

The man shook his head. "No need to tip us. The boss has us covered."

Jake frowned at that, but the man motioned to his

coworker and started walking toward the door. "Bon appétit."

"Mommy, let's pray so we can eat," Lara whispered as the men left.

Cat realized that both Jake and Max were sitting at their places and hadn't touched their silverware or napkins.

"It's only polite in other people's houses to—" she began.

Max interrupted. "Go ahead. We pray all the time."

She could tell the older man felt a little awkward and that it probably wasn't completely true about the praying. She looked over at Jake.

"Would you do the honors?" he asked.

She looked at him carefully. Even with the smile he had managed, he sounded reluctant. Was he cynical, as well? She couldn't tell. When they'd known each other as teenagers, neither one of them had given much thought to God. Finally, she just nodded and bowed her head. She waited so everyone had time to get used to the idea. The last one to bow their head was Jake, but he eventually did.

Then she began. "Father, we are grateful for all of the good things You give to us. We ask Your blessing upon those wonderful men who prepared our food. And we ask…" She paused because she felt a sudden sharp pain in her side and needed to wait for it to pass.

"And please bless my very own father, wherever he is." Lara rushed to fill in the silence with the words that had become part of her bedtime prayers lately. She'd never said them at the table until now.

Cat couldn't get her breath back enough to stop her.

Lara had been curious about her father ever since she realized most of the other children in her preschool had one of those as well as a mother in their families. She had told Lara she had a father, but that was all.

"I figure he's busy like You are, God," Lara continued, with her eyes closed and her hands pressed tight together. "Ruling his kingdom and saving the lives of little children. But can You tell him I said hello and that I'm having a birthday party and it's not even my birthday and if he wants to come, he can ride his dragon here real quick, and I won't tell anyone I'm a princess because he's my father and—"

The pain finally passed enough for Cat to speak, so she quickly finished the prayer in a strained voice. "In Jesus's name, we thank You for all Your bounty. Amen."

Cat sat there for a moment with her eyes still closed. A better mother would have taken Lara to a child's psychiatrist by now. She should have found the money to pay somehow. It couldn't be natural to believe so strongly in something like that. Especially not the tale she'd made up about her father.

When Cat finally opened her eyes, she saw that Jake was looking straight at her, his eyes glowering.

She looked over at Lara. Her daughter was absorbed in eating her macaroni.

When she glanced back at Jake, he'd turned to stare at Lara, too.

"Have you ever seen a picture of your father?" he asked the girl.

She shook her head. "But I know what he looks like. He's a handsome prince with clothes that shine in the dark and he has a beard and he rides a dragon when he takes toys to little kids who don't have any. And I think he invented pizza because everybody loves pizza."

"He's very busy," Jake muttered.

Cat thought he looked a little stunned.

"That's why he can't come to my parties," Lara said somberly. "I wish he would. Just once."

"I'm sure he would come to all of your birthday parties if he knew where you lived." Jake's voice was pinched and maybe a little angry.

She couldn't blame him, but she didn't want him to go further so she shook her head at him. The effort cost her as a burst of tiny pains radiated from her neck.

She noticed Jake's eyes deepen again.

"Problem?" he asked quietly, his eyes measuring her.

"Nothing to worry about."

She hoped that was true. She looked down. Jake saw too much when he wanted to. He'd always known when she was hiding something. Except for those first two months when she was pregnant with Lara. She knew he hadn't known anything about the baby they had created back then. They were too young to get married, and she knew he'd insist on that.

She forced herself to focus on the food that had been placed on platters or in bowls. Everyone was silent for a good ten minutes while they ate.

"Maybe your brother should spring for crab cakes at his wedding," Max said with a sigh as he ate the last one on his plate. "That should fit in his budget, even if he and your mother are fixing up the ranch."

"I doubt anyone makes crab cakes in Dry Creek," Jake said.

"They might if they tasted these." Cat lifted the last bite to her mouth. "They're delicious."

"I don't suppose there's time to get any crab cakes made up before Saturday night, anyway," Max said.

Cat stopped with her fork halfway to her mouth. "The wedding's this Saturday?"

Her timing always had been bad. It was Wednesday. That must have been where Jake had been going when she stepped inside the lobby here.

Jake nodded. "When you said you could stay through the weekend, I called my brother and told him that I can't make it. He threatened to disown me, or at least have our mother call me back, but he knows he needs to get someone else to stand with him."

Cat had never considered that she would come all this way and Jake might not be here. She had thought about calling, but she didn't have a phone number and figured she'd have a better chance of convincing him to spend some time with Lara if he could actually see her.

"You have to still go," Cat said, trying to keep the despair out of her voice. She didn't want him to resent her and Lara. "You're the best man."

"Thank you," Jake said with a grin.

He looked like a carefree rogue and her heart almost stopped. He was the Jake she remembered.

She forced herself to focus. They weren't teenagers anymore. "No, seriously. You have to go. Maybe I could get a room until you get back. I have the whole week off and I can ask for some more days if I need to—that is, if you're coming back soon."

Dear Lord, I need help, she prayed in panic.

"You're welcome to stay here if you want," Max offered immediately. "We don't have a pool, but there'd be no charge for the room. And there's a vending machine on the—"

"Don't get her started on vending machines," Jake interrupted. "She should come with me. I've got lots of room in my pickup."

She thought he looked a little startled at his invitation, as though he hadn't planned it before he offered. She wanted to tell him that he didn't need to worry about them, but pride was a luxury she couldn't afford any longer. "Lara and I would be happy to go with you."

Max pushed his chair back from the table. "Well, as sorry as I am not to have you both staying here with me, that's the perfect solution. I'm going to get some matches so we can light the candles on the cake."

Fortunately, Jake didn't ask any more questions. She half expected him to withdraw his suggestion, but he didn't.

Thank You, Lord. Cat almost said the words aloud, she was so relieved. There would be time for Jake to get to know their daughter. *Please, help him love her like I do.*

Chapter Three

Something wasn't right, Jake told himself for the second time that day as he drove his pickup under the overhang in front of the hotel and pulled it to a stop. An hour had passed since he left. He watched the rain drip off the side of the awning as he struggled to figure out what was wrong. The same sense of unease had been niggling away at him all the way to the airport and back, but he didn't know what was causing it.

Everything seemed to be in order, he finally told himself as he turned off his windshield wipers and then the ignition. The sky was still overcast and the air felt damp inside his cab. Nothing seemed out of place.

He'd gotten the claim tickets from Cat to retrieve her luggage so he knew he had the right suitcases. He'd even stopped at the dealership where he'd bought his pickup several months ago and they had given him a special child's safety seat for the back of his extended cab. They'd strapped it in and he had picked out a green frog-shaped lollipop from the ones they offered and left it for Lara on the seat. He hoped it was close enough to a toad to make her giggle.

Then he'd filled his vehicle with gas. His duffel bag was tucked behind the passenger's seat. His suit was in a garment bag, hanging on the hook by the rear window. He had a wad of cash in his pocket and a credit card in his wallet.

He thought a minute longer. Check and double-check. Everything was ready. Nothing was out of place or forgotten. He opened the door on the driver's side of the pickup and stepped down to the slick pavement. At that moment, Cat pushed open the hotel door and stepped outside. Strands of her brown hair trailed across her face and she looked tired as she took a step toward him.

Jake turned so he could open the rear door to his pickup. Then he stepped toward her. "Have you been sleeping okay lately?" he asked.

She nodded, her teeth chattering. She was wearing the same green sweater she'd had on earlier and it didn't look thick enough to keep anyone warm. He was surprised she hadn't planned better for the trip. A quick check on any of the weather sites would have told her rain and cold were forecast for this area. He didn't think she had even a heavy coat with her.

He suddenly realized what was troubling him. Nothing had been planned about all of this. His intuition was right. A man should never count on random luck. There was always a reason for everything. And Cat coming to him now had no reason that he could see. She hadn't even written to tell him they'd had a baby four years ago. What had changed in all that time? Why had she come now?

Jake looked at her. "Anything I need to know?"

She stood there, her face damp from stray raindrops and her hair limp.

Even as worn out as she looked, she was beautiful. He didn't want to wonder why she was here. He'd love to believe his charm had brought her back after all of these years. Her eyes were not looking at him, though, and that meant something was wrong.

"I haven't been sending you enough money," he finally said, making a guess as he reached for the bills he'd just put in his pocket for the trip. She was too proud to ask, but she must need something. He pulled out a wad of fifties. "I can stop at my bank again on the way out of town for more. Just let me know how much."

"I'm fine," Cat said with no emotion in her voice. "You've already sent me more money over the years than I could have expected—so, thank you."

Then she looked up at him and smiled.

"Still, you must need more," he insisted, watching her. She was too pale. "I refuse to let you live on those noodle cups. They wouldn't keep a bird alive."

After she'd run away from her first foster-care home, she had lived on the streets of Fargo. Sometimes she had jimmied vending machines in the bus station and stolen the noodle packets if she was really hungry. Then she'd gotten hot water from the coffee machine and had dinner. She only permitted herself to steal the noodles if she hadn't eaten for a few days and then she went back as soon as she could and left the payment in the suggestion box at the station, saying it was for the vending-machine guys. He wondered how long she'd gone this time without eating.

"You do remember those noodle packets?" he prodded further, because she hadn't answered.

The Cat he remembered would tell him to mind his own business about now. But she just kept smiling. She was trying too hard to show him that everything was all right. If he didn't know her so well, he would believe her act. But she had a little too much blush on her face. And her smile was too wide. And she moved as if her body ached.

"Had the flu recently?" Jake tried again. Obviously Cat wasn't anxious to tell him what was wrong, but something was. Maybe she hadn't been able to work for a while and was short on money. Or maybe Lara needed braces or ballet lessons.

Cat shook her head and just stood there.

Jake had learned a few things from playing poker. He knew how to recognize a bluff in all its disguises and the emotion flashing on her face might as well have been a scarlet letter. There had to be a reason why she was here. She just didn't want him to know. And she felt bad about it all at the same time.

"You want a new life," Jake finally guessed in defeat. What else could it be? The day wasn't so grand after all. It was starting to rain heavy again and he felt foolish for having rushed around getting them ready for a trip that might not happen. "You wanted me to meet Lara because you feel I have a right to that much, but you're getting ready to marry some man you've met and you're not planning to give me much more than today. So this is my one shot at seeing her."

"Huh?" She was huddled just outside the backseat of the cab and she had one hand on the bars of the car seat. The rain was beating steady on the overhang above them.

"Who is he?" Jake demanded to know. Even if Jake couldn't be a proper father to Lara, it still rankled that some other man would be standing in his place.

Just then a streak of lightning flashed across the sky and there was a loud clap of thunder.

"Who is *who?*" Cat repeated with a frown. "What are you talking about? I hope you have a heater in this pickup."

"It's brand new. Right off the lot," Jake assured her, and all of the fight went out of him. He was going to mess this up; he knew it. But it certainly wasn't Cat's fault. And every girl deserved a father. No one would have to look far to find a better one than him.

"It's nice." Cat reached over and ran her hands across the leather seats.

Finally, he let his bitterness fade away as he remembered. "Not like that old pickup I used to have at the home. I had to put an old blanket over the front seat so the springs didn't poke through quite so much. You'll be comfortable in this one. I promise."

She smiled at him and he knew she could still picture the beat-up old thing, too. Of course, how could anyone forget it? The red paint had been scraped off one whole fender before he even bought it. The side window hadn't rolled up for the previous two owners and the heater barely worked. But he'd been proud as could be of that old pickup. He'd driven Cat into town for dinner the day he closed the deal and the pickup could have been a Jaguar the way it made him feel.

"I wonder if Millie's Café is still there," he said, lost in the memory of that night long ago.

She nodded. "I ate there a few months ago. They still have those barbecue beef sandwiches we used to like. The ones with the dill pickles on the side."

"You were at the home?" Now, that surprised him. They'd both vowed never to go back there once they managed to leave.

She nodded. "I wanted to get some of my records from when I was a resident."

"They must have told you I was looking for you." Jake found he couldn't let the subject go. The only reason he'd gone back to the home was to try and find her. "Why didn't you come see me then? Or call even. I made sure they had my phone number at the home."

"I was…" She started and stopped. She looked so miserable he felt sorry for her. Then she continued. "It's not what you think. There isn't a man in my life or anything like that. I wouldn't keep you from seeing Lara even if there was."

The elastic band around Jake's chest relaxed. He didn't know how they'd resolve this, but he was glad she hadn't already replaced him. He stepped closer and lifted her chin so he could look her in the eyes. She smiled at him now and her eyes deepened. This was the Cat he knew.

"I want to be in your life." He could hear the rain hitting the awning overhead and for the first time it sounded gentle as it fell. "And Lara's life, too. Just a little bit. I know we can't tell her. And I know you're probably worried that I'll turn out like my father, but I promise I would never raise a hand to either one of you. I—"

"Oh, I never thought that," Cat said. She looked genuinely horrified. "I never thought you were like that. I know you would never do anything to harm someone."

Her eyes looked at him with a sincerity he couldn't question.

He nodded in relief. "Anything else we can handle, then."

She didn't answer him, but he figured they had settled the big questions. She was letting him be a part of Lara's life. And hers in some way. For now, that would be enough.

He cleared his throat to say how grateful he was, but she was already turning.

"Speaking of Lara, I better go get her," Cat said, as she started walking back to the hotel lobby.

Jake looked through the glass windows and saw Max bringing the girl to the door. She was carrying a white box that he guessed held what was left of her birthday cake. Knowing Max, he had packed some plastic spoons and napkins in the paper bag he was carrying out to them, as well.

"Now you call me when you get to Dry Creek," Max said as he led Lara to the pickup.

Jake figured he was talking to all of them even though he was looking at the girl.

"We'll probably call you before that," Jake said as he held up his cell phone to remind Max. "You won't even have time enough to miss us."

"See that I don't," Max said as he turned to the backseat.

"You got your own special chair there," the older man said to the girl as he lifted her up to the car seat. "I'll let your fa— I mean, your mother buckle you in."

Lara squealed when she saw the lollipop and grabbed it. Then she looked at Jake and grinned.

"A frog for you to kiss," he said, feeling more pleased with himself than he should.

Lara giggled at that. "I'll make him a prince."

"You sure will," Jake said.

Max stepped back and Cat moved close to the door where she could reach the car seat.

"Don't open the lollipop yet," Cat said as she started buckling the girl in. "You just had all of that cake."

Max shifted beside Jake. "Sorry about my slip."

"Don't worry," Jake assured him. It was hard to keep the news contained. It was like fizz in a bottle that had been shaken up and was looking for someplace to go. Then he leaned closer to his friend. "They'll visit us again."

Max nodded. "Good, because I can't think of anything else."

"I won't be a real father, of course." Jake felt obliged to tell the older man.

"Why not?" Max demanded.

Jake shook his head. "We'll talk about it when I get back."

He looked at the frown on his friend's face. Maybe he needed to say more.

"I'd be a terrible father," he added, his voice low so that no one but Max would hear. "And, you know, Lara thinks her father is a prince somewhere who rides on a dragon taking gifts to poor people. Even a mortal with a normal childhood would have a hard time competing with that. So, it's best this way."

"I don't think—" Max started and then stopped when Jake raised a hand in caution.

By that time, Cat had finished adjusting all the straps on the car seat so Lara was both safe and comfortable. Cat closed the door on the backseat and started walking around the pickup to the passenger seat.

"We'll be back in no time at all," Jake said, trying to keep the tone of his voice even.

"You should have good roads to Salt Lake, at least," Max said as Jake opened the driver's door. Then the older man put his hand in his back pocket and pulled out an envelope. "I almost forgot. You won't need a stamp for this now."

"Thanks." Jake took the envelope and threw it into the passenger seat as Cat opened the door. He looked up at the older man and saw him smile before he stepped away from the cab window.

"What's this?" Cat said as she slid it over so she could climb in and sit on the seat.

"It's yours," Jake replied.

Cat didn't pick up the envelope, but she did move it so it didn't fall off the seat.

Jake settled himself behind the wheel. He figured she knew what was in the envelope since her name was on it.

By then, Max had stepped back to the lobby door and had turned to wave at them as Jake started the pickup.

"It'll be dark by the time we get to Salt Lake," Jake

said to Cat as he started driving. He turned onto the street in front of the Starling. "We should make good time, though."

The leather on the seats was softer than Cat had thought when she'd touched it earlier. The warmth of the blankets made her drowsy. She'd been so tired lately. First it was all the doctors and then flying here with Lara. Being with Jake made her feel as though she could let go of some of the burden and, before she knew it, her eyes drifted closed. The next time she opened them it was dark outside. She saw the red taillights of a string of cars ahead of them.

"Where are we?" She was groggy but tried to sit up straight.

"We passed Salt Lake City a half hour ago. It's about seven in the evening."

Cat had only meant to close her eyes for a moment. She turned to glance in the backseat and saw that Lara was soundly sleeping in her car seat.

"She's fine," Jake said. "I asked her to be quiet so you could get some rest."

"You didn't need to do that," Cat protested, still facing the back. She studied her daughter's peaceful face. "Lara's my responsibility."

"Not completely. Not anymore."

Cat turned around and sagged against the seat at his words. Relief flooded over her. She hadn't even had to ask. He was accepting their daughter.

"Thank you," she whispered.

"You don't need to thank me."

The lights from a passing car shone in the cab for

a second. Shadows lifted from Jake's face and she felt
the urge to reach over and touch his cheek. His expression was so solemn, though, that she didn't dare.

"I still appreciate it," she said quietly, wondering if
he would remember this conversation later.

"It's my duty," he added, and she felt her heart
squeeze. "Just let me know how much you need."

"You mean money?"

"Of course."

Money would never be enough. She could not leave
Lara with him unless he came to love her. Duty wasn't
enough. Not when her daughter had just started to believe in happy endings. As she faced her possible death,
only one thing was important. She wanted her daughter
to live with hope and love in her life. She wanted her to
have something as close to a fairy-tale life as possible.

"I've been thinking about it." Jake turned to her and
smiled. "Like Max mentioned, my mother and brother
are both living on the family ranch now. How do you
want me to introduce you to them?"

"What?"

"An old classmate? Someone from the home?"

"Do we need to say?"

"My brother will pester you to death if he thinks
there's any chance you would marry me," Jake continued with a grin. "I'm not sure I would wish that on
anyone. He has this fantasy about me getting married
and settling down on the ranch. He's even got a hill
picked out with a place to build my house."

A shot of pure longing went through Cat. "Would
that be such a bad life? To live in Dry Creek?"

Jake was silent for a moment, the darkness hiding any expression on his face.

"Years ago I would have said it would be a fine life." His voice was strained. "But after all that happened to my family there, I'm not sure I could live in the community."

"You're not responsible for your mother killing your father."

"Oh, but she didn't." Jake turned to look over at her. "I forgot you didn't know. She thought my older brother, Wade, had done it and, when the prosecution wanted to call him to the stand, she confessed to stop them. She didn't want him going to prison if she could help it."

"Oh, my." Cat let that sink into her mind. She could understand how a mother would do that. "You always said you didn't think she had killed him."

Jake nodded. "No one listened to me."

Another minute went by before he continued. "Those people sent my mother to prison and she hadn't even committed any crime except trying to look out for her son. They heard the Stone name and just assumed she had done it."

"But she told them she had. And Wade—did he?"

"No, he didn't do it, either," Jake said curtly. "That's why it's so upsetting. Those people couldn't see past their prejudices. If they had worked harder on looking at the evidence—or the lack of it—our family would have stayed together and everything would be different now."

The cab was completely dark. There were no lights from cars pulling up behind them. But Cat reached out anyway and ran her fingers softly down Jake's cheek. "I'm so sorry."

He reached a hand up to capture hers and turned it so he could kiss the inside of her palm. Then he curled her fingers around the place where his lips had pressed. "You're a good friend to me, Cat Barker."

He released her hand and she brought it back to her lap.

"That's what I'm going to tell Wade," Jake announced suddenly. "You're my best friend and he'll just have to let go of his curiosity."

Cat nodded and blinked. She had no right to tears. She didn't even want him to say she was his girlfriend. She had nothing to offer Jake except Lara, anyway. It had to all be about their daughter.

"My mother is going to love Lara," Jake continued, as though he could read her mind. "She won't need to think she's related to make a fuss over her…" Jake stopped. "It could have all been different. I should have never let you run away from that home. I should have made you marry me."

"And what would we have done then?" Cat asked. She had been through all that in her mind over the years. "Neither one of us had a job. Or any reason to think we could get one. We hadn't even graduated from high school. All you had was that old pickup and it didn't run half of the time. We didn't have a way to make a life together. Besides, you didn't want to get married."

She thought she had buried the anguish of those days, but it still vibrated inside her. She had never been as scared in all of her life as she had been when she realized she was pregnant.

"At least I could have taken care of you better," Jake replied, his tone tense. "I could have found some kind of a job. I have a strong back. I could have dug postholes or something. Even if we didn't stay together, we should have made it legal. What did you do alone?"

"Mrs. Jenna—you remember the nurse at the home—she sent me to another home for unwed mothers. I had a doctor's care. And learned how to take care of a baby. It was the best thing."

"And did the home suggest you not tell me about the baby?"

Cat nodded her head in the dark. "I'm sorry if that hurt you, but one of the conditions of staying was that I couldn't talk to you. It was a silly rule they had at the home."

"You could have told me later."

Cat closed her eyes and whispered, "By then, I thought you knew. When I got the first envelope of money, I figured you had to have been told by someone. And you never sent a letter. I thought you didn't want to hear from me."

"I always had a return address on those envelopes."

Cat heard a rustling in the backseat.

"Mommy."

"We'll talk later," Cat whispered to Jake before turning to their daughter. "How are you, pumpkin?"

"I'm hungry."

"We'll stop someplace," Jake said, passing an exit.

"We could just get something at a gas station. I don't feel like going into a restaurant and sitting down."

"Usually a gas station only has hot dogs at this time of night."

Cat shrugged. She didn't have the energy to persuade him otherwise. She just hoped her money held out until she could get back to Minneapolis. She was determined to not open the envelope of money he'd laid on the seat before they began. She had moved it to the cup holder between their two seats. If it was charity, she didn't want it.

He pulled off at an exit that had a fast-food sign.

"I'm going to meet your mother," Cat finally said, suddenly realizing what that meant. "And I didn't bring a dress."

One thing she knew about Jake was that he loved his mother. He'd written to the woman often from the home and Cat had envied him having someone. She couldn't even remember her mother. She had a grandmother who had taken care of her until she died. Then Cat had been out on her own.

"My mother's not that way," Jake protested. "Even before prison she didn't care what people wore and…" He broke off and swallowed. "At least I don't think so. I haven't seen her for a long time."

Cat let that sink in. "You haven't been back since she got out?"

A moment went by before he answered.

"I've been meaning to—it's only been two months since she got back."

He paused then, and finally admitted, "I just couldn't face it."

Cat nodded. She could see him now that he was driving under street lights. He had always been as much of a fairy-tale kind of a person as their daughter. He didn't get many miracles, but that didn't mean he didn't want them. Jake fought injustice and didn't like anything to be halfway. She supposed he didn't know how to forgive the people who testified in his mother's trial or the others who didn't intervene to correct mistaken impressions. Maybe he couldn't even forgive himself.

"You could not have stopped what happened," she said. "The judge made his decision. There's nothing you could have done to make it come out different. And, you told everyone who listened that your mother couldn't have hurt a fly. You told me about it. You tried."

"I didn't try hard enough."

He looked tired and not just because he'd been driving for hours. She remembered his smile more than anything else, but she hadn't seen him use it much in the time she'd been with him. Had his mother's situation really changed him so much?

"God will help you forgive yourself," Cat whispered. She wasn't sure she should have said it until the words escaped her. His face froze at her words and he stared straight ahead.

"I know. He helped me," Cat continued.

She wondered how normal teenage girls handled the guilt of getting pregnant. If she had been more careful, she might have had a future with Jake. Lara would have been born at the right time, when she had enough diapers and layettes to stock a proper nursery. Everything about Lara's young life had been a compromise. She didn't have both of her parents or any kind of security.

"Lara doesn't even have a college fund," Cat muttered, half to herself. There was so much to remember before she had surgery. Not that she had much to put in a fund like that, but she wanted Lara to know her mother had thought about her future.

"Yes, she does," Jake said. "I opened one for her when I stopped at the bank on my way back with your luggage. It's in my name still because I didn't know her social security number, but it's waiting for her."

Cat started to cry. She didn't want Jake to see the tears, but she couldn't help it. She had been so worried and so alone for so long. And now Lara had a college fund.

"I won't tell her about it," Jake said low and urgent. He looked over at her. "I know I can't take over. Don't want to, either. You're a wonderful mother."

"That's not it," Cat said, trying not to hiccup. She always did that when she cried. "I'm just so happy you even care that she goes to college."

"Of course she should go to college." Jake's face lit up in a smile as he gave her a quick glance and a wink. "She got her brains from you. She'll want to put them to good use. Maybe save the world someday."

With that, he pulled up to the drive-in and stopped by the order window.

"Hamburgers and fries?"

Cat nodded. Maybe everything would work out for Lara. She was doing everything she could to get her daughter settled in with Jake. She could only pray that God would do the rest.

Chapter Four

Jake had counted off the miles to Dry Creek by the number of stops they had made going north on the I-15 freeway. It had been hours since they'd eaten those hamburgers. They stopped once again in Idaho Falls for gas. And then another time at the old mountain café on the top of Monida Pass just this side of the Montana state line. And now, their last stop was right here in Billings. He looked up at the cliffs that stood high above the east side of the city. He'd pulled his pickup into a parking lot and was admiring the way the rising sun turned the cliffs rosy.

"I forgot to get a wedding present," he muttered to himself, suddenly remembering the fact.

He looked over at Cat, who had to be awake even if she was still curled up against the passenger door. He'd been planning to stop at one of the stores on his way out of Las Vegas and buy a toaster or maybe an electric can opener, but he'd completely forgotten about it when Cat and Lara had shown up. He glanced behind him. Lara was asleep in her car seat.

He had finally found a music station that played soft

rock and the sound filled the cab as he sat there letting the knowledge that he and Cat had a daughter wash over him. It was terrifying and wonderful at the same time. He hoped he didn't do something to disappoint the girl if she ever did learn that he was her father.

"How could you forget a wedding present?" Cat asked as she sat up straighter and stretched her arms. "It's your brother. You should have gotten them something weeks ago. People put a lot of thought into wedding gifts."

"Yeah, well…" Jake began and then shook his head to get rid of the vision that had come to him of Cat lounging like a little calico kitten in the morning sun. She clearly liked the warmth of the heater in his pickup. He wondered if it was because she'd spent so many cold nights when she was on the street as a kid. She finished stretching and brought her arms down to her sides.

He forced his mind back to the conversation. "I'd hoped to talk my brother out of getting married, so I figured there was no reason to buy a gift. I didn't want to be stuck with either a toaster or a can opener if he backed out. But it looks like they are going forward, so I need to get something. What do you think?"

"A can opener isn't very special."

"And the toaster?"

Cat just shook her head.

"Well, then, maybe a new wallet." Once, when they were growing up, Jake had wanted to get Wade a nice leather wallet for Christmas. They had both liked hand-tooled leather, mostly when it came to saddles. But even a wallet had been too expensive for what little money he'd been able to save. "I could slip in a few silver dollars or something."

"A wallet for a wedding?" Cat protested mildly. "I mean, some money is nice even if it's impersonal, but the main gift is supposed to be for both of them. The groom and the bride. And you shouldn't try to talk anyone out of getting married. It's already scary enough without that."

All thoughts of wedding presents fled Jake's mind and he felt his body tense. "How do you know how scary it is to face getting married?" Jake asked, trying to keep his voice calm. "You ever been engaged?"

As much as he had worried about Cat over the years, he'd never pictured her getting married to someone until today. He'd always worried she was alone and hungry, not hooked up with another man.

"If you count the five seconds I was engaged to you, then yes, I thought about getting married," she answered tartly. "Of course, you've probably forgotten all about that."

Cat's chin was up again and it made him relax.

"How could I forget? It was over so fast I had whiplash. You said yes and then stomped off. I thought we would talk about it like adults the next day, but you were gone."

"Well, it was for the best."

"We've already covered that," Jake said and looked in the backseat at where Lara still slept. "Do you think you'll ever tell her?"

Cat didn't answer for a moment. "I don't want her hurt."

"Me, either."

They were both silent after that.

"I should get her some birthday presents," Jake finally said. He was willing to keep his mouth shut about the fact that he was Lara's father. But he felt an urge to do something.

"She doesn't need anything. And you certainly don't owe her for past birthdays."

Jake decided he was going to ignore that. "Maybe I should get her some kind of jewels or something. Rubies or garnets. The simple ones."

"She's only four!"

"And she thinks she's a princess. Little girls like jewels. Look how she wears that crown of hers."

"Those are just bits and pieces of colored glass. The whole thing only cost a dollar. Don't worry," she said. "Lara knows you've been sending us money for years. You're her hero—Uncle Jake, we call you. I already bought that plastic crown she has with that money. And her ballet shoes. And more glitter than you want to know about. And I always say it comes from Uncle Jake's money."

"She calls me Uncle Jake?" In the list of all the things Cat had recited, this was the only fact that stuck in his mind. "Won't that confuse her later? I mean if she ever found out the truth."

Of course, he reminded himself. She already thought her father ruled some fairy-tale kingdom, so even if they told her the truth about him, she might not believe it.

"I doubt she's even tried to figure anything out. She doesn't know about family structure. She's only four," Cat said.

"And three months," the sleepy voice came from the backseat of the pickup and stopped all of the conversation in the front. "Are we there yet?"

"Soon," Jake said as he took a deep breath. "Would you like something to eat?"

"I could have a piece of my cake," Lara said. Her voice gained strength at the thought and she sat up straighter in her car seat. "Grandpa Max packed me my own fork and—oh—" her voice trailed off "—I forgot. I wasn't supposed to call him that. It's supposed to be a secret."

There was silence for a moment as they all considered this.

"Do you know what a grandpa is?" Jake finally asked. He had turned around by now so he could see her clearly.

Lara nodded her head vigorously. "I do, too, know about families. A grandpa is like a grandma only he doesn't bake. No cookies or anything. He buys you cake instead, though, so it's okay. And he lets you slide in your socks on the bare floor. I can go as fast as I want. Grandpa Max said so."

"Sounds like you had fun," Jake said cautiously. He hadn't realized what a minefield this would be with Cat, and he didn't want to cause her any distress. He didn't have any right to a relationship with Lara and he didn't want Cat to think he was overstepping his bounds. Not that, technically, he was the one to bring up the grandpa idea. He should have known Max wouldn't be able to contain his excitement, though.

"How much did you hear before you woke up?" Jake asked.

"What mommy said about families. The other kids in my school have families," Lara said then, her voice a little wistful. "I know he's not a real grandpa, but…"

Jake didn't know what to say to that and, when he looked over at Cat, he saw she wasn't sure, either.

"I never had any cousins," Lara continued piteously. "Or brothers and sisters or aunts or a daddy…" Her voice trailed off, but after a moment she brightened. "I did have a snake once, but he got away."

"I'm sorry about that." Jake felt bad. He couldn't give his daughter much, but perhaps… He looked over at Cat. "Maybe, if your mother doesn't mind, I could—"

Cat shook her head. "Don't even think about it. We can't take care of a pet. And then there are the vet bills and the food and everything."

"I don't think a snake goes to a vet." Jake didn't have the nerve to mention he wasn't thinking about a pet. He had suddenly wanted to assure his daughter that, for good or bad, she did have a father. At least for the record, he was the one. Fortunately, Cat hadn't seen him go close to that edge.

"I could feed it some of my cake," Lara offered. She was wide-awake now and seemed to have forgotten about all the family members she didn't have. "And if I can't have a snake, a puppy would be nice."

Cat turned around in her seat so she was facing her daughter. "You know we can't have any kind of a pet in our apartment. It's against the rules. And no pet ever eats cake."

"But it's birthday cake," Lara said, undeterred. "Everybody eats birthday cake."

For the first time, Jake noticed that his daughter had

the same stubborn jaw that he saw on Cat's face. And when Lara closed her mouth and lifted her chin slightly, he knew they were in for some hard times ahead.

"Why don't you both come with me and we'll look around the stores," Jake offered. He imagined that's what a real father would do. "You can both help me pick out the wedding present for my brother. That will be fun, won't it?"

"Your brother?" Lara asked, her chin dropping a little as she pondered things. "Is he my uncle, too?"

"No." Cat gasped.

Jake could see she was horrified.

"We don't even know him," Cat continued, obviously struggling to keep her voice calm. "You mustn't call him that."

"We didn't know Uncle Jake, either," Lara answered reasonably. "Or Grandpa Max. But now we do. And Grandpa Max wants to be my grandpa. He said so."

"That's different," Cat said as her eyes looked up to meet Jake's.

He read the plea in them and did the only thing he could think of.

"Let's go to the jewelry store." He smiled at Lara. "I'll buy you something special."

"A puppy?" Lara asked before her mother could protest.

Jake chuckled as he shook his head. "Not this time, sweetheart."

He held his breath after the endearment, but Cat didn't quite seem to have heard it.

"She doesn't need anything in that jewelry store." Cat didn't say it with any force to the words. Maybe because she was looking at him with confusion in her eyes. "I didn't come here so you could buy things for her."

"I know, but I wish you had," Jake said, and with that, he opened the door of his cab. A shopping cart full of presents was the one thing he could give Cat and their daughter. He couldn't hurt them by doing that, at least.

Fifteen minutes later, Cat stood in front of a display of goblets in the jewelry store. Classical music was playing in the background and the faint scent of lavender filled the place. Large plateglass windows let generous light into the area. She was used to shopping in thrift or discount stores. She'd never seen so many beautiful things before in her life.

Her gaze kept going back to a pair of elongated glasses sitting on top of the case that held the diamond rings. She took a few steps closer. Those glasses sparkled and she stopped a good two feet away from their shelf for fear she'd smudge them somehow just by staring. One goblet was for the bride and the other was for the groom. She supposed they were for the wedding ceremony and not the marriage that followed, so they wouldn't be a good wedding gift, but they were beautiful. Each goblet had a figure etched on the glass and they were dancing, the bride with her dress swirling wide on one glass and the groom with open arms on the other. Both had their faces tilted up.

"They're lovely," she whispered as Jake walked over. He had taken Lara to get a drink of water in the back of the store.

"I'll buy them," he said with no hesitation.

Lara was looking up at him in awe. Cat knew her daughter seldom heard those words in a store and never without someone asking the cost first.

"I didn't mean they would be good for the present," Cat said. "They're really more something a bride would get for the ceremony. Or a good friend of the couple would give them when they got engaged."

Jake picked up the bride's glass and turned it over. "Made in Ireland. Should be good quality."

"Be careful," she cautioned. "They're expensive. Maybe even Waterford crystal."

Jake didn't slow down at that.

"We could get them, even if it's not a usual gift," he said as he offered the glass to her, questioning whether she wanted to look at it closer.

She shook her head. "I just like the way the artist made their heads turn to each other—that's all."

At that, Jake picked up the groom's glass, too, and brought them together as though he was toasting with them.

"They're kissing," Lara whispered from below as she looked up

Cat nodded as Jake made the lips of the glasses touch again.

This time, when he held the crystal out to her again, she ran her fingers over the bride's goblet. The glass was smooth and cool. It felt elegant.

"We should definitely get them then," Jake persisted. "They're a work of art. The woman at the counter said that some of these things in here will be handed down from generation to generation. My brother is all into family these days. He'd like that."

"They are lovely," Cat agreed.

Jake looked into her eyes for a second, just long enough for her to think she should look away. His dark eyes always held secrets, but she didn't want to know them. For if she did, he would expect to know hers, too. It was too soon to tell him everything.

Suddenly, Jake turned to face a different aisle in the store.

"I think it might be better to get one of those little crystal trays over there," he said, putting the goblets back and turning away from the moment just as she had.

He walked away, speaking as he went. "My brother and his wife can use a tray like that for all the children they're planning to have. Holiday meals at their house will be something. And who doesn't need a place to put their olives and pickles? Generations of the Stone family like olives. My dad was as anti-Christmas as they come, but we always had olives on that day."

Cat was relieved when Jake went over to look at the small tray. She needed to catch her breath. A wave of longing had started clutching at her when they were all looking at those goblets and it was almost too much for her when Jake was staring into her eyes. She wanted to live long enough to pass down some fine glassware like this to her daughter. In all of her possessions, she had nothing special to leave to Lara. Even more than leaving her an heirloom, though, she wanted to dance at Lara's wedding. Was that asking for too much? Cat thought she had made her peace with what her life was to be or not be. It was in God's hands. She knew that. She accepted that. But...

She looked down and saw Lara staring up at her with concern in her young eyes.

"I'll buy the glasses for you, Mommy. I have my piggy bank back home. It rattles real good now. I have lots of money."

Cat pulled her daughter to her. "It's not that, pumpkin. I'm just thinking about what a big girl you're getting to be."

"I'm four and a half," Lara agreed proudly. "Almost, anyway. Two more months."

Cat smiled. She wanted so much and she had no guarantee of anything. She squatted down and hugged her little girl. "I just want you to have a happy life. Remember, if anything happens, I wanted you to have a good life."

"Does that mean I get a puppy?" Lara said, her voice growing bright.

Cat laughed as she stood up. "No, I'm afraid it doesn't. We still have to go back to Minneapolis and live in our apartment and you know there's no room for a puppy."

She sensed Jake behind her before he spoke.

"Do you have to go back there?" he asked.

She spun around to face him. "What?"

He looked cautious. She knew that look. His shoulders hunched over a little and his eyes, black with emotion, didn't hold hers for long. A ripple of tension showed along his jaw, but then he shrugged. "I'm beginning to think that an apartment that doesn't allow pets might not be the best place for you and Lara. Maybe you should move closer."

"Closer to what?" Cat asked in bewilderment. He looked suddenly shy and she didn't understand why. She couldn't afford to drive much farther to work. And rent wasn't cheap in Minneapolis. Her landlord gave her a break on the price because she'd been there for a few years now.

"Closer to me," Jake said quietly.

At those words, Cat's world flipped over. At first she thought he wasn't going to meet her eyes, but then he looked at her squarely and she saw the tumult of emotions in them. For a wild moment, she wondered if maybe she and Jake had a chance to go back in time and be together again. She'd give almost anything to feel his arms around her again.

"I wouldn't try to push myself into your lives. I promise," he said after a moment. "I just—well, if you were closer I wouldn't worry about the two of you so much."

"Oh." Cat felt all of her wild imaginings fall back to earth with a thud. She had somehow forgotten how responsible Jake felt for everything and everyone. Of course, he would want to do his duty by her and Lara. She had come armed with that knowledge. And, truthfully, she was hoping he did feel responsible for their daughter. She just knew that love was a far cry from duty and she had searched for love her whole life.

She had looked away when she heard his words, and he stood still. She knew she had to force back her tears and answer him. He did care enough that he deserved a polite response. She looked at his eyes and saw the emotions had all been wiped clear from them. He was measuring her, but he was distant.

"That's so thoughtful of you," Cat said and forced herself to smile. She concentrated on the faint stubble on Jake's cheeks. "I appreciate it. But my job is in Minneapolis and our apartment is comfortable." She wondered if she had stretched the truth on that. "It's small, of course, but we manage."

"I see," Jake said as he partially turned away.

She resisted the urge to reach up her hand and run her fingers down the length of his cheek like she had with the goblets.

"I'll just go pay for the olive tray," Jake said. His back was facing her fully by now and he was going down the aisle.

"I'll go out and get Lara buckled into her car seat," Cat said as she reached over and took her daughter's hand.

"The pickup's not locked," Jake said from where he stood, looking at the crystal trays.

Cat nodded even though he couldn't see her. She let her daughter lead her out of the store and into the sunlight in the parking lot. Tears were nothing more than a nuisance when a woman needed to walk somewhere. If she kept blinking back the tears, though, she assured herself, they would go away. She hadn't expected Jake to want to be closer when she came so she had no cause for disappointment.

She needed to remember she had come here for Lara. Her own feelings didn't matter.

She looked down at her daughter. Cat needed to be strong for her.

Chapter Five

He had blown it again, Jake told himself as he waited at the counter for the woman to ring up his purchases. He never knew when to keep his mouth shut around Cat. He hadn't meant to practically propose to her. It's just that, when he heard her say their apartment didn't allow pets, he knew that she and their daughter should move closer to him. He hadn't said any word about marriage, but that's where his mind had been going. He wanted to take better care of them. Cat must have known what he was going to say next. She turned so white he had been afraid she was going to faint on him again.

"Four hundred and twenty-three dollars," the clerk informed him with a brisk smile.

Jake pulled his credit card out of his pocket and handed it to the woman.

Cat had always known his intentions before they were clear to him. That was probably why she had bolted all those years ago. Of course, if he had known she was pregnant he would have tracked her down until he found her. If she didn't want to get married, he had told himself, he'd be content just knowing she was okay.

It would have been a fool's compromise, he admitted as he signed the credit-card slip. Even without Lara in the picture, the thought of Cat disappearing again was painful. They needed him—this woman and his child. If nothing else they should have his money in a more settled way. What if he died? Who would take care of them then? His blood ran cold at the thought. No, he needed to be able to picture them in his mind with a house of their own and a backyard with a little black-and-white puppy.

"Sir?" The clerk's voice interrupted his daydream.

"Oh, thank you," he said as he took the large silver bag the woman had been holding out to him.

Several white boxes were nestled inside. He had bought the olive tray for his brother and new sister-in-law, a strand of what the clerk called "starter" pearls for Lara and the wedding goblets for Cat. As he walked over to the door of the store, he wondered if he'd ever be able to give the glasses to her, though, as nervous as she was about any talk of the future.

The sunlight made him blink when he stepped out of the jewelry store. He could see his pickup in the corner of the parking lot and Lara and Cat were inside. The sound of his boots on the concrete sidewalk kept pace with his thoughts as he walked over to his vehicle.

Lara smiled at him through the side window as he got close and he grinned at her before glancing over at the front passenger seat. Cat tilted her head back and it seemed as if she put a pill in her mouth. She followed it by lifting her water bottle to her lips.

He opened the driver's door then. "Headache? I can go to one of the other stores and get some aspirin while we're here."

Cat waved his suggestion away, although her color was still pale. "I'm fine. I just took something."

"I'll be ready to go in a minute, then."

Jake stepped back and opened the large toolbox that stretched across the truck bed under the back window. He quickly tucked the bag in the corner right next to his new set of screwdrivers. Then he closed the top and put the key in the padlock. He didn't want Lara to peek if he left the bag on the backseat of the pickup.

He hadn't closed the cab door completely and he realized the temperature of the air inside the vehicle had gone down by ten degrees while he was stowing his bag of gifts.

"Sorry," he muttered as he swung himself up into the seat and pulled the door closed behind him. "I let more of the heat out than I thought I would."

Cat didn't answer.

"It won't be long to Dry Creek now," he assured Cat as he turned the key in the ignition and started his pickup. He was worried about her.

A grateful murmur came from the passenger side this time, but Cat didn't move her head to look at him. She kept looking down at the floorboard and her hair formed a shield that hid her face.

"You're sure you're all right?" he asked as he let the pickup idle. Maybe she was still sleepy, but it seemed more was wrong. "We can stop and get a hotel room for a few hours if you need to lie down for a bit. I'm sure Lara could use a nap, too."

Cat shook her head. "I'm fine. We need to keep going."

"We'll stop and have breakfast in a minute."

Cat nodded at that, so he figured that's what he needed to do. He had noticed a bright red billboard when he drove into the parking lot. It had invited people to have breakfast at the café ahead and, once he had driven the pickup out to the main street, he followed the sign's arrow to the next intersection. Eggs and bacon would do them all some good.

The café had cinnamon French toast instead, and Cat said that sounded good to her. Jake followed her lead and Lara wasn't about to be left out. The waitress bought them three plates with toast topped with pats of butter and a packet of maple syrup on the side.

Jake was the first to finish his. "That was good."

Cat nodded in agreement, but didn't stop eating to say anything else.

The silence was nice, in a way, Jake realized. This must be what it was like for regular families. No one was taking their plate out to the porch so they wouldn't have to listen to the man of the house rant about everything from the waste in government to the dust a neighbor made plowing his field. And no one needed to stay behind in hopes of protecting their mother from the man's fists when she didn't bring him his whiskey bottle as fast as he wanted.

Jake wondered if those kinds of scars ever left a man.

He could come to welcome mornings like this. There was no tension between anyone at the table. If something needed to be said, they'd say it. But they didn't need to worry about what would happen if someone wanted to pass the salt and accidently bumped their father's hand as they tried to reach the shaker.

"My mother will feed us again when we get to Dry Creek," Jake said and Cat turned to him at that.

Now that she'd had breakfast, her face had more color to it. It was still pale, but the pink was shining through. He'd always thought she had the most beautiful skin.

"I don't want your mother to go to any trouble." Cat sat her fork back on her plate.

"It's too late to stop her," Jake said cheerfully. Things had to be better at the old ranch house now that his father wasn't around. "And she probably started airing out the bedroom upstairs after I called."

Suddenly, a knot formed in his stomach. He'd forgotten. He'd been in such a hurry when he told his mother he was bringing a couple of friends that he hadn't said they were a woman and a little girl. He hadn't pictured until this moment what a difference that made to the scenario in his mind. He'd warned Cat about Wade being likely to make a speech welcoming her to the Stone family. But he hadn't thought about his mother's reaction. She was likely to read more into Cat's presence than his brother would. The combination might scare Cat so far away he would never see her again.

"My family is a little different." Jake figured he better do some damage control now. He shifted the knife on his plate nervously. "We didn't grow up like everyone else. I thought you should know that before you meet them."

Cat sat up straighter at that news and actually looked over at him. "You're not still talking about the murder charge, are you? Because you said your mother didn't do it."

She stopped and glanced at Lara, but the girl didn't seem to hear.

It was silent for a moment as the waitress came by and gestured to Jake's empty plate. He nodded for her to take it.

"And I think she's pretty remarkable for trying to save her children that way," Cat said as she sat there looking troubled about something. "She must be some mother."

"She's not a matchmaker like my brother," Jake said. "You don't need to worry about that. But she'll fuss over you."

"I'm just wondering if I could do what she did."

Jake had never seen his mother as heroic. She had been too quiet for that, enduring rather than confronting things in life. "I think she felt guilty for not leaving my father when he turned so…" He glanced down at Lara, who seemed to be listening now. "When he turned into a bad man."

"Like a troll?" the girl asked.

"Something like that, I guess."

Lara seemed satisfied and turned her attention back to her plate. "My father, the prince, should have been there. He knows how to fight trolls."

"Does he, now?" Jake said. Even the best of mortal men would disappoint his daughter, and he was nowhere close to being that.

Everyone was quiet for a moment.

"So, who did it, then?" Cat asked after a minute.

"The—you know—the deed that—well, stopped your father."

Jake shrugged. "It seems like a neighbor was the one."

There wasn't much else to say after that and it wasn't long before they had left the restaurant and Jake was back on the freeway, driving. Soon the houses of the city were left behind and farmland spread out on both sides of the road. There were great endless swatches of dried grass and old wheat stalks that had been cut short in the harvest last fall. It was too early for anyone to be plowing the fields, so they sat empty, but Jake felt something inside him come to life.

His brother had been right about one thing in their conversations lately. Jake did miss being on the ranch. There was nothing to compare with the feel of a horse under a man as he galloped after a stray calf. And, sometimes, when the sun set on him in Las Vegas, he missed the peace of an evening on the ranch in a way that was almost physical. It seemed as if the love of the land was something born into all of the Stone children.

"I will say for my father that he never took out a loan against the ranch," Jake said because the thought came to him in the silence.

"Some alcoholics would have," Cat agreed. "You have to give him credit for that."

"That's about all he did right."

Jake wondered suddenly if his mother had been to visit the cemetery behind the Dry Creek church recently, where his father was buried. He'd asked Wade a couple of weeks ago and his older brother hadn't gone by. His younger brother, Tyler, was nowhere in the area, so he clearly hadn't looked in on their father's grave. The last Jake had heard about Tyler, he was in a special-ops unit in the armed forces. No one even knew what country he was in.

"There are no words on my father's gravestone," Jake confessed. Something about the vastness of this land made him want to share with her. "He's been buried there for ten years now and no one has even bothered to put his name on the marker."

"Well, I suppose people know who is lying there," Cat said softly. "I wouldn't worry about it."

He quickly glanced over and saw the sympathy in her eyes. He was glad to see that the color in her face was even better by now.

He gripped the steering wheel tighter. "It's not that. None of us know what to say. We can't say he was a beloved husband and father. I'm not sure it's accurate to even call him a husband. What got him killed in the end was that he was having an affair with a neighbor. I suppose we could say the father bit, but it's only true in a biological sense. My brothers and I aren't proud of the fact that he sired us. We talked about it some, just us boys, while our mom was having her trial, but we just couldn't come up with any words."

Cat reached over and put her hand on his shoulder. "There's still time."

"Maybe we could say he loved the land he was born on, although that sounds kind of small to sum up a man's life. Like he didn't have sons and a wife. And people around here would know we were shorting him. An epitaph needs to have some words to it."

Jake decided to talk to Wade about it. After the wedding, of course. No one would want to talk about his father at the wedding, least of all the groom.

It was silent again. Lara had gone to sleep in her car seat.

Cat dozed for a bit. Her medication had strengthened her pulse and she was doing better. She needed to have her talk with Jake soon, though. She wouldn't be able to wait much beyond his brother's wedding. She needed to know with absolute certainty that Jake would give Lara a home if necessary. That was all that was important now.

Just then, she saw a small green highway sign that said Welcome to Dry Creek. Jake pulled off onto a rough asphalt road. The sky met the flat land and in the distance there was a cluster of buildings. She used to love listening to Jake's stories about this small town, but it had seemed larger than life back then. She never pictured it being so tiny in the midst of all the empty land around it. She'd grown up as a street kid in big cities, so she was not used to seeing the sky meet the ground the way it did when there were no trees or buildings to stand in the way. For a moment she felt a little lost and then she decided she liked it. It lifted her spirits to see so much sky.

"How far is your ranch from Dry Creek itself?" she asked. "I remember how you used to talk about this place all the time."

She suddenly realized there wasn't another vehicle on the road, not behind them and not ahead of them, either. They were miles and miles from traffic. She didn't even see a bicycle or a pedestrian. There was a bird of some kind flying low ahead, but that was it.

"I missed Dry Creek back in the home," Jake admitted as they passed fields of dried grass, one on each side of the deeply rutted road. "But not as much as I did later when I was sitting in my hotel room in Las Vegas. I used to sit and wonder how tall the grass was in the summer and how high the snowbanks were in the winter and whether or not anyone was sitting around the old stove in the hardware store and, if they were, what they were saying."

"Maybe you'll move back someday." Cat schooled her voice so it didn't betray her eagerness. If she could choose any life for Lara, it would be for her daughter to grow up in a place like this. Who wouldn't want to have neighbors who knew each other well enough to share gossip? And to live among people who stayed where they were born would be wonderful.

Then she saw it.

"Oh, my." Cat sighed. Here was the final piece she couldn't resist.

Rising up in the distance, on the roof of a small white church, was a short sawed-off steeple. It didn't go as high as it should, but it added dignity to the building. There weren't many trees elsewhere, but there were some around that structure. Rectangular windows lined the side of the place that she could see. Most likely there were windows on the other side, too.

Jake turned to look at her with a question in his eyes.

"It's the church. It's beautiful," she told him.

"That's the one building that's always got a fresh coat of paint." Jake shrugged as though he didn't understand it, his eyes back on the road. "I will say that much for it."

"That's because people care," she said, her voice lifting in triumph. "I can't wait to go there and sit with everyone in a place like that."

She felt Jake apply the brakes until he stopped the vehicle completely. Then he took the key out of the ignition and turned to look at her. His eyes were black with panic and his jaw was set in a rigid angle. "I don't go to church. Maybe my mother and brother will be going. But I couldn't go with you and Lara. I just want you to know that up front. I mean, the wedding will be there. But that's it."

"Oh."

"I could drive you into town, of course." His hands still gripped the wheel and his knuckles were white in doing it. "If you really want to go."

"Won't people expect you to be there? I thought everyone went to church in places like this, even ones who don't…" She stopped, unsure how to proceed.

"Even ones who don't believe?" he finished for her, his voice flat. "Well, in my case, no, they won't expect me to come. I've never been to church in my life."

"Never?" Cat whispered, her dreams crumbling around about her. How had she gotten so caught up in the fantasy of life in a small town that she had forgotten how Jake felt? "Don't you believe in God at all?"

"I'm surprised you even need to ask," he snapped back, finally turning to her. "There's a God all right, but He let my mother go to prison for something she didn't do. And He let my father terrorize his own family. He even let the man kick our dog so hard he broke the poor animal's neck. I was five at the time. Lara's age. So, yeah, He's probably there, all right, but He sure doesn't have much time to spare for the likes of us."

The pickup was silent when he finished. Both of them just sat there.

"He never promised anyone their life would be perfect," Cat finally whispered back.

"Well, He got that much right."

Cat suddenly realized she wasn't the only one with a damaged heart sitting in this cold pickup. Her problems might be physical, but Jake's were just as real—and maybe just as painful.

"Do you know if the church has a prayer meeting?" she asked quietly.

"I expect they do." His voice was tired now, but he put the key back in the ignition and started the vehicle again. "The people in Dry Creek are real big on praying."

Cat nodded, but didn't say anything. She needed to be around people who had faith. Anything was possible when God's people came together and begged for His mercy.

"Mommy?" The voice came from the backseat and she turned around to smile at her daughter.

"Sleep okay?" she asked.

"I had a bad dream," Lara said.

"It'll be all right," Cat assured her. Her daughter had been having an increasing number of bad dreams in the past two weeks and she wondered if some of her own tension was finding its way into her daughter's mind.

"'Cause you're with me." Her daughter completed

the phrase Cat usually used to comfort her. "And the two of us can do anything when we're together."

Tears formed in Cat's eyes. She couldn't promise that anymore and hadn't said those words since she'd had the first tests on her heart.

"God will be with us," she whispered instead.

Jake shifted gears into a slower speed. He didn't glance over at her, but she could tell what he was thinking by the muscle that tightened along his jaw. She held her breath, expecting him to say something, but he was silent.

After a minute, Cat turned back to her daughter. "We're going to be in Dry Creek so I want you to stay close to me and not get lost."

"No one gets lost in Dry Creek," Jake said with half a laugh. "If you're not at the café, you're at the hardware store or the church. Not many places to get lost in. And there's only one street. Not even many trees to hide behind."

"I see a gas station," Cat said as they came closer to the town.

"Must be new since I've been here." Jake paused and then continued, "It's been ten years since the day they hauled me and my younger brother out of this place."

Suddenly the enormity of the weekend was clear to Cat. Not only was his older brother getting married, but Jake was returning home.

"You should have come back earlier," she said without thinking.

"I didn't know what to say to people," Jake admitted. "And my mother and brother have both changed. I wasn't sure I'd fit here anymore."

"Everybody changes," Cat said.

"I never wrote to her. Okay?" Jake's words burst forth, his agony fresh. "I let everyone in the home think I was writing her letters, but they were all blank. All those years my mother was in prison I only sent her one Christmas card. One card in ten years and all I said was to have a good Christmas. I was ashamed to have her for a mother. How do you go home after that?"

Everything was silent for a moment.

"I make a big deal about saying she was innocent back then," he continued. "But I didn't stand by her, either. Not after the verdict. I'm no better than anyone else in this place."

"Maybe you should give her the olive tray, then," Cat suggested with a smile. "It might make you feel better. You know, olive branch."

"Me?" He turned to her with surprise in his eyes.

She shrugged. "I figure she's just happy you're coming home now. She wouldn't want you to stay away because you feel guilty about anything in the past."

"You think so?"

She nodded, a lump in her throat. "Mothers will do almost anything for their children when it comes right down to it."

Cat told herself she couldn't let the tears fall. Too much was at stake.

Lord, what a mess we all are, she prayed. *Help Jake to give his burden to You. And help me to do the same. Lara is Yours to care for as surely as she is mine. Have mercy on us all.*

Chapter Six

Jake stopped in the middle of the strip of asphalt that made up the only street in Dry Creek. His brother assured him he was welcome in this place, but he wasn't sure. The roadside area was dirt scattered with clumps of dead grass and nothing but only a few weeds grew. A couple of old pickups were parked next to the café. Across the street, he could see into the large window at the front of the hardware store. Inside, old farmers were huddled around the potbellied stove, probably complaining about the price of wheat.

A handful of houses were set farther back on each side behind the businesses. Fortunately, it wasn't raining so the ground had not turned to mud. No travel magazine would ever visit this part of the world, but the place twisted itself around Jake's heart anyway. Maybe this is why he never warmed up to those big neon hotels in Vegas. He was a humble man who liked to live close to the earth. But he had stopped at a poker table when he was traveling through Las Vegas and won enough to make him stay.

He looked over at Cat and saw her looking back at him.

"I don't know whether to open these doors or put the key back in the ignition and go somewhere else," he finally said ruefully. "This old place is…"

He stopped, not sure what he wanted to say.

"Home?" Cat finally said softly with a smile on her face.

Jake was startled. He wasn't so sure he'd go that far. "Maybe it's just familiar."

Then, out of the corner of his eye, Jake glimpsed a movement. He looked up and there she was—a gray-haired woman walking right down the middle of the road toward them, carrying a cane in one hand and a big white purse in the other. She must have come out of the café while he was lost in thought. It was chilly and she had a brown wool coat on, with a flutter of red-and-white gingham dress showing beneath it. He knew he couldn't hear the sound of her white orthopedic shoes, but her steps were certain, with or without that cane. It was the set of her shoulders that told him who she was.

"Mrs. Hargrove," he whispered and the years rolled backward. Maybe he had come home.

For all of the problems he had with the rest of the people here, he had nothing bad to say about this one. She'd sent him and his brothers birthday cards each year, no matter where they were. And she'd always tucked a worn five-dollar bill inside, along with a verse of Scripture she'd written out by hand. She was partial to the Psalms of David, when it came to him.

"That's the woman who wanted you to go to Sunday school that time?" Cat asked, her voice puzzled.

He'd forgotten he'd told Cat about Mrs. Hargrove years ago. "She said she'd give me a piece of apple pie if I'd go for just one Sunday. Just forty-five minutes. And I think she mentioned whipped cream, too."

"I'm surprised you didn't do it."

He grinned as he glanced back at her. "I was a man of principle, even back then."

A soft rustle could be heard behind him and then Lara spoke. "Does the lady still have some pie? I'd go to Sunday school if she wanted."

"I expect Mrs. Hargrove always has pie," Jake said as he twisted around far enough to see that Lara's wide eyes were looking straight ahead at the woman.

"She looks kind of funny," the girl finally said, as if she was trying to figure something out.

"You'll like her," Jake assured her. "All of the kids do."

Just then there was a tap on the side of his pickup and he turned back to roll his window down.

"Well, don't just sit there, Jake Stone," the older woman scolded as she grinned up at him. "Get out here where I can give you a hug."

"Yes, ma'am." Jake opened his door and stepped down to the asphalt.

He stood there, feeling suddenly awkward.

"My, how you've grown." Mrs. Hargrove looked him over carefully, pride shining in her eyes.

"It's been over ten years," Jake reminded her. He almost thought she was going to check his ears to see that they were clean, but she didn't.

"Too long—that's all I can say," she announced. And, with that, she stepped closer and gave him the hug.

He smelled talcum powder and felt the bony strength of her arms. Just about the time he felt tears start to burn behind his eyes, the older woman gave him an extra pat on the back and stepped away. Her own eyes were suspiciously bright.

"Your mom said you were bringing some buddies to the wedding," Mrs. Hargrove continued, the expectant look on her face hard to miss now that the he wasn't in the shadow of his pickup.

Jake realized the sun had been too bright for her to see inside his vehicle, especially since his windows had a slight tint to keep out the glare.

He turned around to the door that was still open to his pickup. It was going to be hard to hide the fact that he had a daughter. Fortunately, no one looking at Lara would leap to the conclusion that she was related to him, because she was blonde while he was black-haired and brown-eyed.

It wasn't that easy, though. He was gripped with an intense desire to tell this woman who Lara was. She would be almost as excited as his mother. Of course, both of the women would never speak to him again because he wasn't married and providing for his child as he should. Those envelopes of cash seemed pretty puny to him now.

"I'd like you to meet Cat Barker," Jake said as he moved so Mrs. Hargrove could see inside the cab better. "And in the backseat is Lara Barker."

"Oh, your mother is going to be so pleased," the older woman said as she moved in close enough to look into the shadows inside the pickup. "When she told me, I said Jake's buddies couldn't be men. Remind her that

I said that. You have to drag men to weddings, but not women—and especially not little girls. They love to come."

Mrs. Hargrove glanced in the backseat before turning to Cat.

"I'm so pleased to meet you." Mrs. Hargrove looked straight at her. "And what an unusual name."

"It's really Cathy."

That made Mrs. Hargrove's smile grow even wider. "Oh, a nickname. That's so nice. My name is Edith and there's not much I can do with that. I just don't seem like an Eddie. And, my husband—" she turned back to Jake "—you heard I got married, didn't you? To Charley Nelson. But I still go by Mrs. Hargrove most of the time. It's so hard for everyone to get used to a new name after all this time, and I keep forgetting, myself. Besides, Charley is fine with it. He knows I love him. It's not the name that makes a marriage, is what he says. Bless his heart."

"Congratulations." Jake wondered if Mrs. Hargrove was blushing or if her cheeks were just pink from the exercise she'd had walking down the street.

"Thank you, and who do we have here?" Mrs. Hargrove leaned farther into the cab of the pickup so she could see into the backseat better. "I'm so pleased to meet you, Lara. You're going to have to stop by my house soon and have a cookie."

Jake could see Lara's blond head bobbing up and down in agreement. Her blue eyes had grown wide.

"I'll go to Sunday school if I have to," the girl said, her voice pure innocence and filled with hope. "I like pie, too."

Mrs. Hargrove's smile turned into a laugh. "I see Jake has been talking to you about when he was a boy."

"I just—" Jake started, but Mrs. Hargrove waved his protest away.

"The offer is still open, you know. In fact, I'll give you the whole pie if you come." She paused. "And your choice of whipped cream or ice cream. With cinnamon sprinkles. They've started using ice-cream sprinkles at the café and everyone in town uses them now."

Lara clapped her hands in delight, and he ducked his head slightly in a gesture that could mean yes or no. He didn't want to disappoint the woman—or Lara—but a man like him had no place in a Sunday-school class, no matter how tempting the bribe. He could picture the bitterness rising up in him if he even tried such a thing. Besides, he'd heard about the little chairs they had in her Sunday-school room. He wouldn't fit anymore.

He saw the excitement in Lara's face, though.

"Cat and Lara might like to go," he finally said quietly. He didn't want to hold them back if that's where they wanted to be. "Sunday is close enough after the wedding and we'll still be out at the ranch so I can drive them in easy enough."

He realized he didn't mind taking his daughter to the Sunday-school class he'd never attended as a boy. All the kids he knew had gone to the class and it had made him feel like an outsider to have never done so, even though Mrs. Hargrove had gone out of her way to invite him many times.

It was quiet for a moment.

"Your mother is going to be so proud of you," Mrs. Hargrove finally said as she stepped back. "But she won't thank me for keeping you here in town when she's waiting out at the ranch. Make sure she puts her feet up, too. She sprained her ankle the other day and isn't resting like she should."

Jake frowned. "I hope she's not working too hard. She shouldn't be doing anything where she could sprain her ankle."

"She was painting the upstairs bedrooms."

"She didn't need to do that," Jake said.

"She told me she did it just in case I was right about your friends," Mrs. Hargrove said. "So, be sure she rests."

"We'll take care of her," Jake promised the older woman as she moved to the side of the road, obviously ready to wave them goodbye as they drove through the small town.

Suddenly, he couldn't wait to get out of Dry Creek. There was too much emotion for him here. His past was going to reach up and swallow him whole if he wasn't careful. He turned the key on the ignition and started driving forward.

"Bye," Lara said, waving wildly as they passed Mrs. Hargrove.

Cat reached over and patted his arm lightly and that lifted his spirits.

He was quiet for a bit.

"Not a vending machine in the whole town," Jake teased as they passed the café.

"I'm sure there's one at the gas station," Cat said smugly. "Every gas station has a vending machine— sometimes two or three."

He'd forgotten about the new gas station and looked

in the rearview mirror at the chrome-and-glass building. It was the only structure in Dry Creek that didn't look a hundred years old. Whoever owned it was wise not to have any surfaces that needed painting. The severe winters around here meant most of the houses always looked as though they were in need of a new coat of paint.

"When we're on our way back through town, we'll stop and see whether or not there is a vending machine," Jake said. "I'll buy you the candy bar of your choice if there is one."

"Me, too?" Lara asked from the backseat.

"You, too, sweetheart."

Jake saw the slight frown that Cat gave him, but he decided to ignore it. He supposed she was upset that he'd called Lara that several times now. But a man was entitled to have a pet name for his daughter, even if the girl didn't know he was her father and so probably didn't understand the significance of the endearment.

He almost braked to a stop when he realized—of course, Cat wouldn't like it when he said things like that. It set a bad example. He pulled to the side of the road and parked before he turned around in his seat.

"I'm sorry, Lara. I shouldn't call you anything but your name." He suddenly felt a clutch of worry. "And no other man should, either."

"Okay," Lara said very matter-of-fact.

"And don't take candy from strangers, either." It was more complicated than he knew, watching out for a child.

Lara looked unhappy at that. "But I want my cookie.

Mrs. Hargrove already said I could have one if I went to her house."

"Yes, well, Mrs. Hargrove is different. You can eat anything she gives you."

Jake was exhausted and he had the feeling he had not made his point clearly, anyway. Fortunately, Cat had been watching him bumble around and took pity on him.

"Just tell Mommy before you take any cookies or candy from anyone," Cat said and then hesitated. "Or tell Jake, and he can decide if you should."

His heart soared. He felt as if he had been promoted to parent. It was a small thing, really. Any adult should be able to assess a threat involving sweets, but it made him feel good that Cat trusted him to do something like this for Lara.

"Thank you," he said to Cat as he looked over at her. Her face was still paler than it ought to be. "When we get to the ranch, you'll have to take a nap. I'm used to driving through in a pickup and tend to forget not everyone does those kinds of things."

Cat looked at him and laughed, her eyes lit up with mischief. "You're forgetting, I lived on the streets for years until I was put in the home. I can sleep standing up against a door with the wind blowing around me. A pickup is the next best thing to a pillow-top mattress."

"Well, I'm going to open a bank account for you when we get back to Las Vegas. I don't want you to ever be homeless again." The thought made a chill go down his spine.

"You've already done so much," Cat protested.

Jake was going to say something, but she continued, "I'm fine. Really."

Jake nodded. He didn't want to argue, especially not about money. He'd find a way to set up an account for her when they got back to Vegas. In the meantime, he'd take her home to the ranch where she'd be comfortable.

They were through the town when he spied the red barn that the community used for the Christmas pageant. He'd heard that the minister's wife had painted a mural on the side of the building that included something in the sky that looked like a denim quilt.

People invested their lives in this place in a way that made him feel lacking. That quilt represented a woman who had buried her husband and then turned his shirts into something. Suddenly, the single life Jake lived in Las Vegas didn't seem as appealing as it had when he left. No one would turn his old shirts into anything but rags if he died.

He glanced over at Cat. He had no business hoping for more.

Cat saw the barbed-wire fence running along the dirt road, but she didn't realize why it was there. The posts looked new and the sunlight reflected off the wire. The fields to the side were covered with dead grass, but it looked pressed down, as though a tractor had been driven over it recently. It reminded her of some vacant lots she'd seen in cities, but the ground seemed cared for at the same time.

"I see Wade's been at it," Jake said, and she could hear the satisfaction in his voice. "That fence needed replacing when we were kids. I expect the next thing you know he'll be running some cattle on this side of the coulee. From the looks of it, there was good grazing here last year. And he probably spread some fertilizer so the grass will come up even higher when spring gets here."

She felt proud just listening to Jake. He sounded like a rancher.

Jake slowed down as they approached a turnoff that led into the fenced area. "Mind if I open the windows? It's cold out, but the smell in these old fields is something else when you drive through—even when nothing is planted yet. I sometimes think the smell of the soil stays pent up all winter and comes alive as things thaw."

"Please, open all the windows you want."

Cat watched Jake instead of looking out the windows. His face never betrayed much, but she could see his eagerness in the way he leaned forward over the wheel and kept glancing from side to side as they moved slowly down the road leading toward some buildings. His hair was slightly mussed, and black stubble covered his face. He'd opened up the collar on his white shirt and he reached up to rub the back of his neck as a sound of pure contentment escaped his lips.

He was a rancher, all right.

She turned to look straight ahead. A two-story house was coming into view and a large red barn was behind it. Both buildings were worn, the paint faded on the barn and obviously chipped on the house. They had some years behind them, no question of that.

"I always envied you this place," she said quietly as she turned to Jake.

"Why?" His voice sounded surprised as he glanced over at her. "You grew up in the big city. Lights. Action. I would think you would have liked that."

"I never had a home," she reminded him. "Not a place like this. I could fall off the face of the earth and not one neighborhood would miss me. I know people here and there, of course, but they're not one community."

She hadn't realized until she said the words how solitary her life had been. She had always felt rootless, as though it didn't matter where she lived. She had no relative but a grandmother. The thought that someone could belong in a place with ties that stretched back for generations was foreign to her.

"Well, I'm sure…" Jake started and then stopped. He frowned slightly and she recognized that expression from school. She understood he didn't want to be glib, but she could offer him no consolation. He didn't know what it was like for her. And, truthfully, it might not bother her if she wasn't worried about what would happen to Lara if she died. She had no family, no community of friends to leave her daughter. No place to even run an obituary where people would read about her life and know who she was.

"We need to get you a house," Jake said then, his voice earnest. "I'm serious. Instead of you just renting, I should buy you a place. With a big shade tree and a backyard for a puppy. And big windows—you've always liked the sun."

His gaze caught hers and she was silent as they kept looking at each other. She wished—just for a moment—that she could tell him everything in her heart. That sunshine might not be enough. Maybe he would understand what it was like to face death without knowing a place where she belonged. She'd given her heart to God, but she yearned for a community on earth that would miss her when she was gone. She might have spoken, too, but a tiny squeal came from the backseat.

She was grateful for the reminder that her daughter was present.

"We'll talk about that later." Cat tore her gaze away from Jake and turned to Lara. She hated to dampen the excitement on her child's face, but she didn't want her daughter to think Jake's words were a promise. People said things when their emotions grabbed them that they didn't remember later. Or sometimes had no way to make come true anyway.

Lara was silent so she turned to Jake. He'd turned his attention back to the road by then.

"A house is a big investment," she said to him. She didn't want to risk being disappointed, especially when it would hit her daughter the hardest. "And I'm fine with renting."

He nodded, but when he glanced over, his eyes were not backing down.

"I've got it covered," he said. "Maybe we should call a real-estate agent."

Cat was going to question him further, but she heard her daughter catch her breath in excitement.

"Doggy," Lara screamed from the backseat and Cat thought she was in for a temper tantrum. She should have stopped Jake earlier. Lara wouldn't understand a broken promise. Cat turned and saw her daughter pointing a finger out the window. Then she saw the dog.

The yellow animal was loping toward the pickup with its tail wagging in welcome. Cat was so relieved the dog was present and not just in Lara's dreams that she sat there for a moment. The wholesome picture of this place was complete when it had a dog that looked like Lassie.

"Is that a collie?" she finally asked.

"Beats me," Jake answered as he eyed the dog, too. "But I'd guess it's a mutt. People around here don't usually have pure-bred anything, except maybe cattle."

The dog started barking then and turned to run alongside the pickup.

"Doggy," Lara repeated from the backseat, and Cat wondered how she would convince her daughter to leave this place when it was time to go. Then she realized her daughter wasn't the only one who would want to stay. A sweep of dirt covered the area between the house and the barn, but at the back of the area, behind an old clothesline, was a row of deep green bushes. She'd seen their shape in pictures.

"Are those the lilac bushes?" she asked Jake softly. She couldn't count all the times she had asked him to tell her about his mother's flowering bushes. And there had to be two dozen here. "They're real."

"Absolutely." Jake gave her a quick smile. "Remember that soap I got you?"

"Of course I do. It wasn't easy hitching a ride, carrying a case of soap with me."

"You could have left them behind."

"Are you kidding? Taking baths with the scent of lilacs all around is what helped me get through my pregnancy." She had felt like a princess using that soap.

"I'm glad you liked it."

She had felt close to Jake when she breathed in the fragrance.

Cat turned away from Jake to look at the bushes again. "The smell of the soap is nothing compared to the real thing, though."

As deep green as the leaves were on the bushes, the flowers would be mature when they bloomed.

"I'm surprised those bushes are still alive," Jake said as he stared at them. "No one lived here for ten years while my mother was away. I guess someone must have come in and watered them a little, at least. I wonder who—"

The sound of a door banging came in the open windows of the cab.

Cat sat up straighter in the seat. A woman had just come out of the house, her long black hair pulled back. She seemed ageless, neither young nor old. She held a hand up to shade her eyes from the sun as she stared at the pickup. She was wearing jeans and, if it wasn't for the cane, Cat got the impression she might have jumped up and down just like the dog was doing. The woman had an expectant angle to the way she was standing, like she was leaning forward. She was clearly watching them draw closer.

"Your mother?" Cat hadn't realized how strong the sun was shining outside until she saw the brightness as it reflected on the metal of the woman's cane.

"Sure is," Jake said, affection warming his voice as he gave his pickup more gas. "And she looks like she can hardly stand still."

"She'd be walking out to meet us if she could," Cat agreed.

Jake nodded. "She's the type that must hate not being able to get around easily. She's always had a mind of her own, except…" He paused for a moment and when he continued the lightness was gone from his voice. "Well, except for when she was around my father, of course."

By the time Jake parked the pickup, Cat could see his mother clearly. She was a thin woman and had the look of someone who had worked hard her entire life. She wore a rose-colored short-sleeved blouse, tucked into the waist of her jeans. Her jet-black hair was pulled back into a knot in the back of her head. Cat wasn't sure, but it looked as though the woman wore a cowboy boot on one foot and a black slipper on the other. Her cheekbones were high and her skin darker than most. It was her Cherokee heritage, she supposed, that gave her the regal look.

It took her a moment to realize that Jake was just sitting there, behind the wheel. He had switched the ignition off and now held the keys in his hands. Finally, he turned to her. "Ready?"

She nodded, surprised at the rush of shyness she felt. "Is my hair okay?"

Her purse was sitting on the floorboards and she reached down for it. She had a small brush in there. And lipstick—she wondered if she needed some lipstick.

"You're beautiful," Jake said simply.

She looked up, her purse in her hand now, and was touched by the expression in his eyes. Golden flecks warmed the black color and it struck her that he was proud of her. She let her purse drop back down to the floor. "I'm ready, then."

Cat opened her door seconds after Jake opened his. She slipped to the ground and stepped slightly to the side so she could open the back door of the cab. She needed to lean inside to unbuckle Lara from her car seat. Even at that, she barely had Lara down by the time Jake made it around to their side of the pickup.

"Okay?" Jake said softly as he touched her elbow.

She nodded, grateful that he was walking with her and Lara. She had wished many times back in the youth home where they stayed that she could see Jake's family, but she had never imagined actually meeting them. They were important to him whether or not he was willing to admit that to himself. Cat didn't know much about having a parent. Her mother died giving her birth and she'd never known who her father was.

She watched the smile grow on the woman's face as Jake brought them forward. Her eyes were as black as Jake's and they both had the same prominent cheekbones. Cat had the impression the woman didn't ordinarily display her emotions, but that she was almost overwhelmed by seeing Jake.

"Oh, I'm so pleased," the woman said when they were halfway to her. She looked at Jake. "Welcome home."

There was no wind and her voice carried perfectly, but Jake didn't respond. Cat stumbled slightly on a clump of dead grass and he reached out his hand to take her arm. He probably only did it to steady her, but she appreciated it. He moved closer, walking on one side of her while Lara was on the other.

Suddenly, the dog bounded up from behind them and raced to the woman.

"Down, Honey," the woman said and the dog sat at her feet, its tail still thumping in welcome. "You don't want to scare our guests."

By then they were close enough for Jake's mother to hold out her hand. She reached for Jake first, but he stiffened.

"I'm so glad you came here with my son," the woman continued, offering her hand to Cat, instead.

"Thank you, Mrs. Stone." Cat took the woman's hand. She felt the hard calluses on the fingers as the woman squeezed her hand in welcome.

"You must call me Gracie," the woman said as they shook. "We're all just family here."

The woman's eyes turned to her son then.

Cat's breath caught, and then she assured herself the woman had merely used a figure of speech. She couldn't possibly suspect Lara was her granddaughter.

Jake's mother looked back to her.

"I'm Cat," she said as they finished the handshake. She stepped back, and Jake took her arm again. Then she realized he hadn't said anything yet. She glanced up at him quickly and saw his face locked in some kind of a mask.

"You must be thirsty," Gracie said, her voice hurried as she wiped her hands against her jeans. "I have some lemonade sitting in the refrigerator for when you got here." The woman glanced up at Jake. "I know how you boys all loved lemonade."

Cat noticed Gracie wasn't looking at Jake any longer and the woman's eyes slid down to Lara as she smiled. "I'm guessing you'd like some lemonade, too."

"Yes, please," Lara said very politely.

Jake's fingers gripped her arm more tightly, but Cat didn't move.

"Well, then," Gracie said in what sounded like relief. "Let's go have some, shall we?"

Cat waited for Gracie to turn and start walking back into the house before she turned to Jake. He didn't look angry, but his face was frozen in some way.

"You okay?" she asked. Lara was already following the older woman.

Jake nodded, but he didn't say anything. He dropped the hand that had gripped her arm and started walking toward the house.

Cat took one last look around the outside of the ranch. The door to the barn was wide-open and some kind of a tractor was parked inside. A new pickup was parked on the left side of the barn, so someone here was as prosperous as Jake.

She almost cried when she saw the water dish by the door to the house that read Honey. She imagined everyone here had their place on this ranch. A shot of pure longing ran through Cat. She wished she had a place here, too.

Chapter Seven

Jake looked around the kitchen of the house where he had grown up. Sunlight was coming in the window above the sink and he saw some repairs had been made where it looked as though rain had come inside. Ten years of standing vacant couldn't have been good for this old house. It had been built by his father's great-grandparents when they first homesteaded here, so the walls were thick and the structure sound enough that it had probably taken the neglect in stride.

It was comforting to see it had been repainted inside. The walls were a cream color and it still smelled the same as it had when he was a boy. He caught the scent of coffee mingling with the lemon smell of some disinfectant. His mother must use the same brands as she had years ago. She'd added red curtains, but the scarred wooden table sat in the middle of the room like it always had. He and his brothers had carved their initials on the underside of the table one night for no particular reason that he could remember now.

Cat had taken Lara to the bathroom upstairs so he and his mother were alone.

"You did a good job painting," he said as he saw the trim on the cabinets and a small mural with a red bird that had been added to the wall. "It's nice."

"Amy Mitchell did the bird," his mother said proudly as she noted where his gaze had traveled.

Amy was the neighbor his brother, Wade, was going to marry. The two of them had been childhood sweethearts and, even though Jake didn't approve of his brother getting married in principle, he did soften when he thought of Amy. She was a good person. He only hoped the family legacy his father had started didn't follow Wade into that union. He'd hate for Amy to be hurt like his mother had been.

Jake watched then as his mother turned with the help of her cane and pulled a large pitcher of lemonade out of the refrigerator. He walked over to help her and then stopped. He felt a sudden urge to open his arms to her, but he wasn't sure she'd welcome a hug.

His mother turned to set the pitcher on the counter and then closed the refrigerator door.

"Let me help," he said as he saw her look up at the open cabinets where the glasses were.

"I can get them," she replied.

He should have written when she was in prison instead of just pretending to do so for the officials of the home. It had been worse for him to ignore her than it had been for his two brothers, because he had known deep inside that she was innocent. She could never hurt anyone, no matter what they did. And when he didn't write, it was like saying he thought she was guilty just like everyone else did.

His mother set her cane against the counter and

reached up into the cabinet. Looking down, he could see her feet. The foot in the slipper was swollen and he started to say something as she set a glass on the counter, but she started speaking before he had a chance.

"I want you to know how very sorry I am," she said as she slowly moved to face him squarely. "I should have been a better mother to you and your brothers."

The surprise of what she said made his eyes turn damp. She looked sincere, her black eyes meeting his with such tenderness that he couldn't question her emotions.

"I'm the one who should be apologizing," he said brusquely, hoping to stop the lump forming in his throat. "You were the best mother, and I didn't even write when—"

He heard a whimper and the dog was suddenly between them. If the animal had stayed in its corner by the door, Jake would have opened his arms at last.

"I should have reported your father for his abuse," she said, waving away his words and continuing with her own. "I had myself convinced we had no choice, but I was wrong. I should have gotten help for us all."

"But how?" Jake demanded as he looked at her. He didn't like his mother taking the blame for something like that. With the sun shining full through the windows, he could see the new wrinkles on her face. Nothing about her stance had changed, but there was a freedom he'd never seen before in her eyes.

He wondered for the first time how she could have come back to this kitchen. It, along with the rest of the house, had been her cage as much as any prison she'd been in later.

"Dad never let you go anywhere by yourself," he reminded her as he gestured around the room. There hadn't even been a telephone in here for most of his childhood. His father had always kept the phone in a closet that he locked during the day. His mother had to ask permission to call anyone. "This was the only place he let you be. How could you have found someone to help us? He hid the keys so you couldn't drive anywhere. The ranch is way out in the country. Even if you did manage to call, by the time a county sheriff got here, Dad would have been passed out so there would have been nothing to see."

Bruises wouldn't have counted for much, he told himself. His father always had some story to tell, and with three boys, most lawmen would have figured they did the fighting among themselves, anyway.

"I could have gone to the church," his mother said. "Your dad would have taken me there even if he wouldn't have stayed. And I could have stood up in the service, asking people to help us. The people there would have banded together. I was so timid that I didn't even try. Some of the men told me they would have helped us handle your father if they had known what was happening."

Jake felt his jaw tighten. He heard the sounds of footsteps walking on the bare floors in the living room. "Yeah, well, it's easy for those men to say what they would have done when the time for doing anything is past."

Those church men had no idea what a force his father had been, drunk or sober. And he wouldn't have liked his mother asking strangers for help.

The footsteps ended at the door to the kitchen, but Jake found he couldn't stop his words.

"The truth is, all any of those men from the church would have done is pray," he finished, the bitterness stripping any softness from his voice. "So they might as well have been spitting in the wind for all the good it would have done this family."

The gasps of the three females around him sucked away his belligerence. He turned around to look at the doorway and saw that even little Lara was shocked. Her blue eyes were big and horrified. He figured he had no hope of being her prince now. She'd call him a troll and she'd be right.

"I'm sorry," he muttered, giving a nod to his mother before returning to where Cat and their daughter stood. "I know you all pray and I'm not saying you don't have the knack for it."

Wade had filled him in on the religious awakening their mother had in prison when she had been in some support group there. Even when he was a boy, she would have taken him to task for disrespecting anything related to God, so he expected her to scold him now. Instead her attention seemed to have gone elsewhere.

"You're a believer?" His mother stepped to the side so she had a clear view of Cat.

"Yes."

"Well, isn't that wonderful!" his mother exclaimed with more animation on her face than he remembered her having at any point when he was growing up. She clearly believed in something that had given her a new passion for life. She didn't even lean on her cane as she looked at Cat.

Life in this house had certainly changed since he'd been here last.

No one needed to remind him that Wade had started going to church, too.

"Of course, I don't mind if people go to church," Jake said, figuring he might as well wave the white flag. He wasn't going to win this battle in this house. "It's just that—well, a man's entitled to have an opinion about prayer."

He didn't feel God should get credit for something He hadn't done, and He certainly hadn't done anything to set his mother or his brothers free from his father. He glanced over at Cat. Her face was too pale again, so he sent her a reassuring smile. He didn't want her to worry about his soul on top of everything else.

Then he looked back at his mother and she had the saddest expression on her face.

"It's my fault that you feel that way," she muttered, half to herself.

"That's not true. It's…" He scrambled to think of something light to say. "It's Mrs. Hargrove's fault."

"What?" his mother asked in surprise. He noticed that she was smiling now, though. "How could that be?"

He saw that Cat and Lara were stepping into the center of the kitchen.

"Mrs. Hargrove only promised me a piece of pie if I went to Sunday school," he said, trying to grin convincingly. "She should have known I'd hold out for the whole thing."

His mother laughed at that, the sound filling the

kitchen with a happiness he hadn't known it could have. He heard Lara's giggle join in after a bit, too. Cat was silent, but she was there. His mother barely stopped when he opened his arms wide and stepped close enough to hug her to his chest.

That's when he heard a satisfied sigh come from behind him and he knew Cat was happy, too. She felt conflict even more than he did and would want him to be at ease with his family. He realized it had been a long time since anyone had cared about him that much.

A half hour later, Cat sat at the kitchen table with an empty glass of lemonade in her hand. Jake had taken Lara out so she could walk the dog, even though he assured her that pets on a farm didn't need to be walked like they did in the city. The window by the sink was open and she could hear Lara's delighted squeals in the distance, mingling with the excited yips from the dog and the deep chuckle from Jake. It sounded as if the three of them were racing around together. Maybe it wasn't the dog but the girl who needed the walk.

The open spaces around the ranch would be good for Lara.

Jake's mother had insisted Cat stay and let Jake take care of her daughter. The truth was, Cat probably couldn't have kept up with Lara if she tried. Not today. The drive here had been almost as much as she could handle. She felt the flutter in her heart just sitting here.

"You look a little tired," Gracie had said as she gave Cat her glass of lemonade before Jake and Lara left.

The sugar had boosted her energy somewhat, but she was barely able to sit while Jake's mother walked around the kitchen, using her cane to steady herself as she moved dishes into the cupboards from the drainer near the sink. The older woman kept up a steady stream of chatter about the weather and what the forecast was for the weekend.

Then suddenly she turned.

"You were the one at the home, weren't you?" Gracie asked as though she had just realized something. She kept the dish towel in her hand as she hobbled over to the table and sat down. "One Christmas when Wade called me, he said that Jake had a special friend there. Wade called the other boys once a year or so. I was so grateful, knowing Jake had someone to talk to. That was you, wasn't it? I remember you had an unusual name."

"I was there, all right," Cat admitted. She tried to deepen her breath. "Right where the state put me. Jake was the one who started calling me Cat because I had said my given name was boring."

"We never like our names when we're that age, do we?" Gracie said with a smile. "I know I couldn't stand to be plain Grace so I had to dress it up with the *ie* on the end of it."

"I like being called Cat."

"You're going to have to tell me all about the home while you're here," the older woman said. "I tried to get Wade to ask his brothers questions, but—you know how boys are—he never managed to find out much. Mostly he just said they didn't like the food. I always worried about Jake. I think he took my going away harder than the others. He always has had such a strong sense of justice."

Cat nodded. The room was beginning to spin slightly, but she didn't want to put her head down to her knees and close her eyes. That's what she usually did.

She pulled herself back to the conversation. If she could just focus, she'd be all right. "Jake does think life should go in certain ways."

"And he gets disappointed," his mother added as she stood up again. "Maybe you should have some tea to go with the lemonade. Or a sandwich. I could make you something. I have a pan of lasagna in the refrigerator that I plan to put in the oven for supper, but a snack would be good."

"I wonder if I could lie down for a few minutes," Cat said as she started to stand.

"Of course." Gracie walked around the table and offered her arm for Cat to hold. "Let me just help you get to my bed—"

"Oh, I couldn't take your bed."

"Nonsense," Gracie said softly. She had the cane on one side of her and Cat on the other as she slowly led Cat out of the kitchen. "My bedroom is the only one on the ground floor and we're not taking the stairs."

Cat didn't argue further. She needed everything she had to keep putting one foot in front of the other. She hadn't realized what a strain the drive up here to Montana would be on her. And the worry of meeting Jake hadn't made any of it easy, either.

"We're almost there," Gracie said as they stepped through the bedroom door.

An impression of white clouds filled Cat's mind. She wasn't sure if it was the color in the room or if she was slipping into unconsciousness. She did see a big window in the room.

"I'll be fine," she muttered as Gracie gently helped her lie down on the bed.

Cat felt the fabric under her. It was a quilt made out of denim. She could feel the ridges of the seams. The fabric was soft as though the material had been worn until it was smooth. She didn't bother to try and keep her eyes open.

"Should I call the doctor?"

Cat heard Gracie's voice from a distance and fought her way back to consciousness. A doctor could spoil everything. She needed to keep her secret for a little longer.

"I'm fine," she said and struggled to make her voice sound reassuring. "Really, I am."

She forced her eyes open and tried to smile. The sunshine was so bright she had a hard time zeroing in on Gracie's face even though the older woman was leaning over her in concern.

"If you could get my purse from the pickup," Cat managed to say. One of her heart pills would help her.

She wondered why Gracie's hands were gripping hers as she tried to surface more completely. And then she realized she was the one holding on to the other woman.

"Have you told Jake that you're pregnant?" Gracie asked quietly.

That was enough to bring Cat completely back. "What?"

Her hands fell away from Gracie of their own accord.

"You don't have to tell me, of course," the other

woman said with a worried look on her face. "But I have had three babies and I fainted a time or two when I carried them. Especially at first."

"I'm not pregnant," Cat managed to whisper.

Gracie just patted her hands. "Well, all I'm saying is that, if you are, you need to talk to Jake. I raised that boy, and he'll do right by you."

"But..." Cat tried to explain, but she couldn't carry it further. Jake's mother was five years too late with her suspicions, but she wasn't wrong in the basic story. Or the fact that Jake had always seen it as his duty to marry her.

Just then Cat heard the door to the kitchen slam shut and the clatter of feet sound on the linoleum floor.

"That will be Jake and Lara back from their walk," Gracie said, her voice warm with some emotion that Cat didn't even want to think about. "You just rest a minute. I'll see that your purse is brought in and I'll fix you some toast."

Gracie straightened up.

"Thank you," Cat murmured for lack of anything better to say. She watched as the older woman turned and used the cane to walk steadily out of the bedroom.

Cat closed her eyes again, but this time it wasn't because she was fainting. She heard the sounds of whispering in the kitchen, first Gracie's low voice and then Jake's deeper answering one. She figured no one would say anything while Lara was there, but the dog would make a good distraction for her if either Jake or his mother decided they needed one.

Cat barely had her eyes closed before Jake came in

carrying her purse and a small plate with a piece of toast.

"I understand you want these," he said as he laid the purse on the bed beside her and put the plate on the nightstand to her left.

He stood there for a moment looking awkward until he stepped over to the wall and brought back an old spindle chair.

"You could have told me, you know," he said as he pulled the chair to the bed and sat down close enough to her head that she didn't have to strain to see him. "I have enough money to help you with two children."

"What?"

"I can see why you might have been nervous about telling me," he continued. "And I hope I never meet the man who is this baby's father, but we can't blame the baby for anything. I'll provide for it."

"There is no baby." Cat almost gritted her teeth as she lifted herself up slightly just to make her point. "I'm not pregnant. I gave my life to God just a few months ago. I'm certainly not running around with men. And I never have. Is that understood?"

She closed her eyes at the end of her speech. When Jake didn't answer, she opened them again. He was sitting there with a grin on his face.

"So there's no other uncle somewhere?" he finally asked.

"No, you're the only *uncle*," she said, exaggerating the word to let him know it was an annoying question. "And it shouldn't matter to you if there was another one."

"Well…" He began his thought and then let his voice trail off. "I'm glad, anyway."

"If you'll bring me some water, I can take that pill I need," she said. She wasn't sure how she felt about the satisfied look on Jake's face. She had always considered it a defect in her character that she hadn't been able to get over him enough to form an attachment to another man.

She must have scowled because Jake got up quickly to get her what she needed.

The room seemed empty without him, but it was more peaceful. She pulled herself up so she was sitting with her back against the pillows. She glanced down and saw that she'd been right about the quilt. Someone had put a lot of hours into piecing old denim squares together. She wondered if Gracie had been the one to make it.

The room was large, but there wasn't a lot of furniture in it. Straight ahead of her the closet doors were closed. A dark walnut dresser to her right held a hairbrush and an assortment of old photos in silver and gold frames. Even one in brass. She supposed they were family photos. A mirror with what looked like an oak handle sat next to the hairbrush and a scattering of bobby pins lay in a white saucer close to the back. A bottle of lilac hand lotion sat nearby. On her left, the window was open and the scent of damp earth came inside through the screen.

She wondered how the room felt so peaceful after what Jake had told her about his father. It would seem as if violence would leave its mark here someplace. Maybe it was the passage of time that had wiped it away. Ten years was a long time. And then she saw a crack in the plaster of the wall by the door. Someone had tried to repair it, but the line was still faintly visible when the sun was shining on it like now. The man was still remembered by the room, after all.

Chapter Eight

Jake stepped into the kitchen and saw that his mother had filled the dog's dish with water and given it to Lara. He wished he had a camera so he could take a picture of the two of them with their heads together, one with her black hair pulled back and the other with golden curls falling all over her neck and shoulders.

"Just put it outside by the door," his mother instructed the little girl as she helped her put her hands far enough under the bowl so she could carry it. "And don't worry about spilling some. It's only water and that's what I have a mop for. Just take your time. Walk slow and you can do it. It's the first step in learning how to take care of a pet."

Lara let out an impatient sigh. "I need a doggie like Honey."

"I know you do," his mother assured her as she patted the top of the girl's head.

"Don't let Cat hear you say that," Jake cautioned with a grin as he walked farther into the room. Lara had already spilled a drop or two on the linoleum floor.

"There's no pets allowed in their apartment in Minneapolis."

At his words, his mother straightened up and faced him. "A child needs something to love."

Lara interrupted her slow journey to the door by turning to beam at his mother.

"I need a doggie," she agreed, before continuing on her way.

His mother waited for Lara to go through the door before saying anything, but he could tell by her indignant stance that the words were forming in her mind while her lips were pressed together.

"That is one precious child," his mother said finally, her voice low and intense. "I just met her and I already feel like I've known her forever. You can't be sending her and her mother back to that place."

He wasn't sure if it was a question or a command.

And then his mother added, "Not when Cat might be pregnant."

"She says she isn't, Mom," Jake answered. He needed to put that hope to rest. "She's not expecting."

"I know a fainting woman when I see one," his mother retorted as she leaned forward on her cane. "She might not have taken a test yet, but—"

Jake shook his head as he walked over to the sink. "She says she hasn't been with anyone. And now that she's so much into God and prayer, I believe her. Well, I would believe her anyway. Cat has never lied to me."

"Oh." His mother's shoulders slumped at little. "I know it's not right when two people aren't married, but I guess I was just hoping that you and she—well, a woman can't be blamed for wanting her sons to have babies she can spoil."

Jake didn't trust himself to answer that. His mother had a granddaughter; she just didn't know it.

"I better get some water for Cat," he said instead as he reached up to grab a glass and started filling it from the tap. When he was finished, he walked across the kitchen floor again. He went through the living room along the path he'd known as a boy. He was careful not to walk on the big rug his mother had near the sofa. He did glance up at the oil painting of the coulee behind their farm that some great-uncle had painted decades ago.

He arrived at the bedroom and Cat invited him in.

When he stepped inside, he squinted. The bedroom had two large windows and more sunlight flooded in here than in the living room. Both of the windows were half open and looked out on the back pasture. He heard the sound of a vehicle driving up to the house, but he couldn't see the road from this side of the house. He wasn't sure if it was the engine of a car or a pickup that he heard. Somewhere in the distance he heard a bird of some kind, too.

He was standing there when Cat opened her eyes and looked up at him. He forgot all about who might be driving to the house. She smiled at him and the feelings he had for her rose up and filled him with wonder and then despair. Seeing her lying on his parents' bed reminded him of the promises of marriage at the same time that it brought up the pitfalls for a woman who was foolish enough to marry a man like him.

"I'm surprised my mother has kept the same bed,"

Jake muttered as he walked close enough to set the water down on top of the nightstand.

"Of course, she's probably not doing it for sentimental reasons," he added as he sat on the chair that was still sitting where he'd left it. "This is the only bedroom on the first floor and, since she hurt her ankle, it's the only one that makes sense for her to use."

"This is her room and always has been," Cat agreed. "I doubt she's changed anything in it. Lying here, it just has that feel of being old. Your father's clothes are probably still in that closet over there. I'm guessing she can't bear to part with them—and maybe she doesn't even realize they are there because she's so used to seeing them."

Jake didn't have the nerve to go and check that out. "I suppose my mother did have some affection for him," he finally admitted. "In the beginning, at least. But things changed."

He realized as he said the words that he was describing the nightmare he hoped to avoid by sidestepping marriage. In the beginning, everything probably had been wonderful for his parents, but his father had carried the seed of some consuming anger in his soul and it all came out. Jake wasn't sure if he'd inherited that seed or learned that same way in his childhood or not. He tried never to raise his voice, at least not much. But he didn't know what he was capable of if he was drunk or caught in the grip of some powerful emotion. He tried to avoid finding out by not drinking any alcohol, but a man couldn't escape all emotions no matter how he tried.

"I doubt my mother felt much fondness toward my

father at the end," Jake emphasized. He'd do well to remember that as he saw the softness in Cat's eyes. The way she was looking at him now was more temptation than any man should have to face. She might care about him, or think she did, and he had to admit that the thought of having her for a wife made him tremble with hope. He didn't have any guarantee she would accept if he proposed, but he knew he'd give his life to protect her.

That wasn't enough, though.

"You know I'd beg you to marry me if I could," he finally said, the words bursting out of him. She deserved to know that. "But I can't risk saddling you with who I might become."

"You're not like your father," Cat answered back, her voice low and serious. She understood.

He stared down at his hands.

"Jake," she called him back with a whisper.

He gave himself permission to look into her eyes. Maybe it was the golden flecks in her green cat eyes that made him feel as if she was looking deep inside him. She almost made him willing to throw common sense away and let the present be enough. But then his eyes followed the delicate lines of her cheeks and her chin. His mother used to have bruises along her jaw on a regular basis along with the black eyes. Beauty could be broken with violence.

"No one knows what would happen, though, do they?" Jake managed to say as he forced himself to stand up. He would never risk that. "I could turn out worse than my father. Children from abused homes often become abusers themselves. I've read that in books."

"But those are only statistics," Cat protested, her eyes darkening. "God is not limited by statistics."

"Yeah, well," Jake mumbled. Now that she had become religious, she was only more vulnerable to foolish hopes and dreams. He started walking toward the door. "I better go check on Lara."

Cat didn't say anything as he left the room and he turned to carefully close the door behind him.

Some dreams were not meant to be.

Jake walked through the small hallway and entered the living room. He heard voices in the kitchen, but he wasn't ready to talk to anyone. He needed a moment alone so he sat down in the stuffed recliner by the large window. He leaned back in the chair that had been his father's. To his dismay, the lumps in the chair fit his body. He'd grown to the size of the man who used to sit here on winter nights and drink himself into oblivion. Jake was surprised he couldn't smell the alcohol. Ten years didn't seem as though it would have been long enough to erase the presence of his father so completely.

He ran his fingers over the tough texture of the chair's brown cloth upholstery and then looked out the window. He saw his mother's lilac bushes. She always said his father had planted them for her when he first brought her to this house as his bride. She had loved those bushes even though she had to tend them every year to bring them through the winter. When they were in full bloom, their scent filled the house and, in season, she would bring tall clusters of the branches inside and set them in glass jars around the house. The fragrance reminded him there had been some days of peace in the nightmare that had made up their lives. The one time he'd seen his father lean over and kiss his mother had been such a day. Maybe that's why he liked to give Cat things that smelled of lilacs.

Jake heard a footstep in the doorway that stood between this room and the kitchen. He looked up and saw his older brother leaning against the doorway, with a grin on his face.

"Wade!" Even though he hadn't seen the man for ten years, Jake had seen enough pictures of him accepting rodeo prizes that he would know him in a dark alley anywhere. His brother had grown into a man from a lanky teenager, but he still had a cocky tilt to his head that marked him as the same.

Jake started to get up from the chair, but his brother waved him back down.

"I don't know how you can manage to sit in that chair," Wade said as he pulled a brown folding chair over that had been sitting by the sofa. "I always keep expecting Dad to come in the room and demand to know what I think I'm doing making myself at home in his chair. Although these metal chairs aren't a joy to sit in, either. The truth is, if he were still alive, I'd be sitting in his chair every chance I got. I think it's him being dead that keeps me away."

A line marked Wade's forehead where his hat usually sat; he must have taken his Stetson off and left it in the kitchen. He had dirt on his denim shirt and a hole in his jeans that looked as though it had been made by catching on some machinery part. The man had been working in the fields somewhere.

"Looks like you've put on a couple of pounds since you left the rodeo," Jake said as he eyed his brother. Wade had the same part-Cherokee coloring that he had.

His brother grunted. "You'd pack on some, too, if you were eating Mom's cooking these days. She says she didn't, but I'm convinced she took cooking classes when she was away."

"Probably just all those cable cooking shows in that place," Jake added. It didn't escape his notice that neither he nor his brother could manage to say she had been in prison. They made it sound as if she'd been away at a resort.

"It's good to see you," Jake said, not wanting to dwell in the past. "I'm glad to be here for your wedding."

Wade looked at him for a moment as though he was waiting for something.

"That's it?" Wade asked. "No more advice telling me I shouldn't do it?"

Jake grunted. "Well, you shouldn't do it, but I figure if I haven't convinced you by now, I'm not going to be able to before tomorrow afternoon. Besides, it's too late to call it off."

Wade smiled slowly. "You're not fooling me. You've gone soft on the subject of marriage. I figured that much out when you showed up here with a woman of your own. Mom told me about her. Says she's real nice."

Jake's grin faded. "I'm hoping you'll go easy on Cat. No kidding her about marrying me or anything. You'll scare her to death."

"Hey." Wade spread his hands. His eyes were amused. "I'm not the kind of guy that would tease a perfectly innocent young woman who just happened to be riding around the countryside with my little brother."

Jake recognized the look in his brother's eyes. "Just remember, I can take you in a fair fight."

Wade laughed. "Since when? You didn't build any muscle hanging around those poker tables, I can tell you that much. I'll ease up on the marriage talk, but I'm not making any promises about not trying to convince you to come back to the ranch. A man can make a life here. Amy and I are going to build a house on the rise over by the coulee, but there's other good places for a house."

"Nobody makes any money ranching these days," Jake said, just to keep his brother talking about the ranch instead of his love life. "Unless you're one of those big corporations."

"Well, at least a man doesn't lose his shirt in ranching like he does in Las Vegas."

Jake just grinned. "My shirt is doing very nicely there."

Now that they were away from the topic of Cat, Jake was feeling pretty good about seeing his brother again. He had never told him how much he won at the poker tables.

"Seriously, you don't need to worry about me and money," Jake said. "I've got enough."

"Well, however much you have, you're going to need more now that you're expecting a baby."

"I told Mom there is no baby," Jake said, starting to

rise. He felt like he was a teenager again and no one believed him about anything. "No one is expecting."

Wade stood up, too. "Yeah, she said you'd say that, too. But she keeps hoping."

Jake shook his head as he finished standing up. "I don't know why she won't believe me."

Wade chuckled as he started walking back to the kitchen. "Claims she just knows you're a father."

Jake froze where he stood. "She what?"

"Didn't I tell you?" Wade turned around. "Our mother gets impressions these days. I think it's from her time away. She also looks for signs from God, so don't leave any baby bottles around."

Jake didn't answer his brother. Wade definitely hadn't told him any of that. He wondered what other secrets his mother saw.

Lord, if I were a praying man, today would be the day. Jake felt the words flit through his mind without him giving them permission. He wondered if it counted as praying if he hadn't intended to say any of it. Finally, he decided it couldn't. He was more comfortable being angry with God than he was asking Him for help.

He did have a sudden urge to go back and check on Cat. He needed some reinforcements if he was going to spend much time with his brother and mother. It wasn't far from dinnertime.

He looked in the bedroom and saw her sleeping soundly, though, so he closed the door and left. She needed her rest.

Cat woke up when the sun was low in the sky and shadows were starting to form in the corners of the room. She had a moment's panic when she wondered where she was and then she remembered Lara. It finally came to her that Jake was with Lara and they were all together at his family's ranch in Montana.

Feeling relieved, she turned to look at the clock on the nightstand and saw that it was five o'clock. She was feeling pretty good. The pill had calmed her heart and she'd slept well.

Still, she shouldn't sleep any longer. She sat up in the bed and looked across at the dresser mirror. Her hair was a disaster and most of it had worked its way loose from the band she'd pulled it back with earlier. Fortunately, she kept a few hair items in her purse.

She swung her legs around to the side of the bed and made the effort to stand. She stepped over to the mirror and used her brush to tuck her hair back up into a casual knot on the back of her head. Her green sweater looked as if she'd slept in it, but there wasn't much she could do about that until she had her suitcase. Before she left the room, she walked back and fluffed up the pillows on the bed and smoothed out the quilt. Then she picked up her purse and turned to leave.

The living room was in shadows, but she knew from the strip of light shining under the door to the kitchen that everyone would likely be gathered there. It was quieter than she expected, though, and she could smell something cooking. Maybe they had all gone somewhere.

When she pushed the door open, she saw that Gracie was sitting at the table with an open Bible in front of her and her head bowed in prayer. A bare lightbulb hung over the table but it was not turned on.

"Oh, don't let me disturb you," Cat whispered as she started to back out of the room. Now that she read the Bible herself, she counted the time as holy when anyone was reading it. She hadn't opened the door before Gracie lifted her head and smiled.

"Please, come sit with me," the other woman said. "Supper's in the oven and I'm waiting for the boys and Lara to get back from their drive down to the coulee behind the barn. They waited for a bit so you could go with them if you woke up, but then they needed to go or it would have grown dark."

"Is it far?"

"It's halfway between our ranch and the Mitchell place where Wade's fiancée, Amy, was raised. You can walk it in five minutes, but Wade wanted to pull a piece of old decking down so he needed the tractor. He's setting up a place to build an outdoor fireplace there for evening picnics this summer."

"That sounds lovely," Cat said as she walked over to the table.

"A man will do most anything to please his wife," Gracie said with a nod as Cat sat down. "Amy has always been partial to sitting outside on a starry night."

Cat nodded as though she knew what that would be like. "The only fires I've seen at night were the ones we had on the streets in Fargo during the winter. Sometimes people would get together and burn some trash in a barrel. We didn't cook anything but hot water, but once someone had a can of cocoa and we made up as many cups as we could."

She wondered if she should have shared any of that when she saw Gracie's face.

"It was nice," Cat added and folded her hands in front of her. She'd said too much but there was no taking it back. It was silent enough that she could hear the clock ticking on the wall by the refrigerator.

"Life hasn't been easy for you, has it?" the other woman finally said as she put a bookmark in her Bible and closed it.

"Please, don't stop because of me." Cat gestured to the book.

"But I might not have another chance to visit with you," Gracie said. "And I want to know that you have enough help."

"I get by." Cat didn't want anyone to feel sorry for her. "I have a job as a receptionist. The best job I've ever had. And then there's Lara. She makes up for a lot."

The sun was setting and pink filled the sky. Shadows were starting to form in the corners of the kitchen.

Gracie nodded. "A daughter like Lara would make up for a lot. She's a delightful child. I had my three boys, but there's something about a little girl that is special."

Cat shifted in the chair. "She believes in fairy tales, you know."

"And she doesn't like peas," Gracie added with a smile. "And she's trying to convince herself she's a princess."

"She told you?" Cat asked. Her daughter didn't confide her fantasies to many people and she was glad Lara felt comfortable enough to tell Jake's mother. "I do try to make her eat just a few peas if that's what's served.

I haven't figured out how to handle the princess thing yet, though."

"Your little one also informed me that she's four years and three months old."

Cat didn't know how to answer. "She's been in preschool, but she starts kindergarten next year."

Gracie just looked at her then as though she was waiting for something. Finally, the woman said, "I figure she must have been born shortly after you left the home where you met Jake."

Cat nodded. She could hardly deny that much, but she wasn't going to say anything more. She told herself she was being foolish, that Jake's mother could not possibly suspect that Lara was his child. The hair coloring and eyes were too different. But she didn't want to rouse the woman's curiosity.

"You must have met someone then," Gracie said. "After you left the home? You would have been a child bride."

Cat willed herself not to squirm. "I wasn't a bride. But it's all in the past."

Just then the sound of a dog barking came through the window. It was followed by the rumble of an engine and a squeal that could only belong to Lara.

"You had to do it alone, then?" Gracie asked. "Giving birth and raising your child."

"Other women do the same," Cat said with a shrug.

At that moment, the door to the kitchen opened and it seemed as if everyone came inside at the same time. Wade reached against the wall and turned the light on as Jake and Lara slid in around him.

Cat blinked in the brightness.

"Supper's ready," Gracie said as she started to stand. "The lasagna's heated and I have a salad in the refrigerator."

"You just sit down," Jake said as he walked over and put his hand on his mother's shoulder. "Wade and I can set the table."

"There's more lemonade in the refrigerator, too," the older woman said as she sank back into the chair. "My foot starts to hurt more toward evening."

"Well, you need to stay off of it," Wade said. "We want you to be comfortable for the wedding. And Amy said to tell you she'll be able to come over later. About eight or so. She's got things to do to get ready."

Then Wade looked at Cat. "I'm pleased to meet you. I'm Jake's brother."

"I know." Cat smiled. "If there's anything I can do to help you get ready for the wedding, let me know. Anything."

"You can convince this guy here that it's okay to be happy at a wedding," Wade said as he chuckled and nodded his head toward Jake. "People are going to wonder what's wrong if he goes around with that dour look on his face."

"I'm not dour," Jake protested. "And, even if I was, it would add some dignity to the day."

"It's a wedding," Wade said. "It's not supposed to be dignified. You have it confused with a funeral."

Cat envied the brothers' back-and-forth bantering. She looked down and saw that Lara was watching them with a fascinated look on her face, too.

"What's a funeral?" Lara asked in the silence that followed.

The question hung in the air as all traces of laughter disappeared. Cat was speechless. She hadn't realized until that moment how little she had prepared Lara for the possibility of her death. She had worried about who was going to raise her daughter if she couldn't. She had debated about writing her a series of letters for her to read on her birthdays, just in case. But she hadn't thought to explain to her that sometimes parents needed to go away. And that, even when they did, they still loved their little girls.

"Well, a funeral is when people get all dressed up in their church clothes and go say goodbye to someone who has died," Jake said.

He looked toward Cat for approval. "Did I miss anything?"

Cat looked at her daughter. "Just that we don't need to be afraid of death. God is in control of that as much as He is of our lives."

Lara nodded. "Do doggies have funerals, too?"

"Sometimes," Cat answered.

"Do they have food at funerals?" Lara asked another question. "I'm hungry."

Cat gave the nod to Jake on this one.

"They do often have food." Jake squatted down so he was eye level with Lara. "But it's not nearly as good as the cooking you'll get right here tonight."

By the time Jake had finished with all of Lara's questions, his brother had brought the dinner plates and silverware over to the table.

"Just tell me where," Cat said as she lifted up the first plate. The other woman pointed to the places where she wanted people to sit.

"I'll get the salad," Jake said as he turned around and stepped closer to the refrigerator.

Wade opened a cabinet drawer and pulled out a pot holder. "I'm going to pull the lasagna out so it can set," he said.

"It smells wonderful," Cat said as Wade opened the oven door.

Cat vowed then and there that she was going to learn how to cook. There was something so right about this family as they prepared to eat together. Even if it was just her and Lara, they would enjoy something cooked at home instead of pulled out of a deli carton.

Wade removed the large pan of lasagna from the oven and Cat's mouth watered as she saw the cheese bubbling on the top.

"Does the doggie get some?" Lara asked as she stared at the pan of lasagna, too.

It suddenly occurred to her that Lara had never seen a family dinner with this much food.

"I have some dog biscuits you can give Honey," Gracie said as she stood up.

"We'll get it, Mom," Jake said as he motioned for her to return to her chair. "Just tell me where."

By this time, both of the brothers had tied white dishtowels around their arms.

"Their father used to do that." Gracie leaned over to whisper to Cat. "He certainly had his faults, but sometimes he helped in the kitchen. Bless his heart."

Cat nodded. She supposed there had to have been some good in the man or he wouldn't have been able to help raise such nice sons. "Do the boys look like him?"

Gracie shook her head. "No, they take after me. All three of them."

Cat didn't know what she'd said, but Gracie's eyes got big for a second.

"Are you okay?" Cat asked the other woman.

She nodded. "I think I just swallowed wrong."

Cat didn't point out that the woman hadn't been drinking or eating anything. She seemed to be doing okay, though. Maybe memories didn't settle too well with her. Cat could appreciate that. She felt as if she had too few memories one minute and too many the next. Mostly, though, when she saw Jake do something like clown around with his brother, she felt as though she'd never have enough scenes imprinted in her mind. She loved to see him happy.

Chapter Nine

Jake pushed back his chair after supper. Night had fallen and the kitchen window opened to darkness in the space between the two red curtains that didn't quite meet. The chatter had finally slowed down, along with the clanking of the silverware, so he could hear the soft sounds of the clock that had hung on the wall since before he'd been born.

He sighed in contentment at being home. The smell of the baked lasagna lingered. The old faucet on the sink, made of that dull metal that wasn't used anymore, had the same slight drip when the handle wasn't turned hard enough. Which explained the old pliers lying on the windowsill. And, there was the dent in the side of the refrigerator where he had hit it with a hammer because Wade had dared him to do it, saying he didn't think Jake had enough power in his swing to make much of an impression. He'd been four years old. Wade almost seven.

The refrigerator hadn't worked at first when his mother moved back in recently, but Wade said she'd had someone come out to fix it—except for the dent, of course, which would stay there until the appliance finally died for good.

He looked around at the people still sitting at the table. The light above shone down on Lara's golden curls, as her head drooped from exhaustion. He glanced up and met Cat's eyes. She smiled and he believed it was because she liked that he kept track of their daughter. He felt like some invisible force watching over Lara even if she didn't know who he really was. He might not be a prince, but he liked taking care of her.

"This is the best meal ever," he said and turned to his mother. "Thank you."

Of course, he wasn't overlooking the fact that it was so pleasant because his father wasn't sitting there with them. Jake just didn't want to ruin the evening by thinking about the man.

"You outdid yourself," he complimented his mother again when he noticed she hadn't responded.

She nodded at that, but still looked at him a little strangely. Come to think of it, she had been quiet during the whole meal. And, now that he noticed, she had half of her food left on her plate.

"Something wrong?" he asked her. "Your foot's not bothering you, is it?"

"I guess I'm just too excited to eat," she said and he had to admit it was not pain that shone from her eyes. She looked like a little kid waiting for Christmas to come even though the Thanksgiving wreath wasn't off the door yet.

"I know you're happy about Wade and Amy getting married," he guessed.

"Yes, that, too." His mother nodded.

Well, he thought, it obviously wasn't the wedding, but his mother didn't say what it was and everyone was silent for a moment.

"Well, who's going to help me wash the dishes?" Wade finally asked as he pushed back his chair. "I think I can get anyone who volunteers a bowl of ice cream after we finish."

Lara squealed and raised her hand. "What kind of ice cream?"

"Mango," his brother said with a grin as he walked over to the sink.

Lara screwed up her face as if she was debating the question. "Manga what?"

"We have vanilla, too. With nuts and chocolate sauce if you'd rather." Wade turned around to add, "I might even be able to find some sprinkles for the top."

"Okay," she agreed and then grinned up at him in pure adoration.

His brother liked his daughter, Jake noted to himself in approval. She seemed to like him, too. Maybe her time with them wouldn't scar her forever.

"I'll help, too," Cat offered as she pushed her plate farther back on the table and put her hands on the table in preparation for standing.

"Count me in, as well," Jake said as he started to rise.

"No." The single word came from his mother's mouth and it stopped them all. Even Wade turned back to stare.

Jake looked at his mother and sat back down. "I'll be careful with the plates if that's what you're worried about. I know I broke that pitcher once, but that was because I was messing around trying to catch a lemon with it."

That had been after the hammer incident and he had been trying to be careful.

His mother shook her head. "I just want to talk to you. And I can't wait much longer."

"Sure," Jake said, wondering what his mother could need to talk about that had her so obviously agitated. Maybe his father's memory was here to ruin the evening, after all. "Is it all the talk of funerals earlier? I know we haven't finished up the headstone for dad's grave yet, but we'll do it soon. We just need to find the right words to put on it."

Jake wasn't sure there were any right words, but he didn't see the need to share that. Maybe they'd think of something.

"Have you stopped by there yet? The cemetery?" Wade asked from his place by the sink, most likely deciding that was their mother's problem, as well. He turned the water on and then glanced back at Jake. "I went by the other day and it needs to have some weeds pulled."

"I'll go over tomorrow," Jake offered. If it upset his mother to see the grave with weeds all around, he'd do what he could for her. His father would not have cared, but then he wasn't much for neat borders in life, either.

"That's not it," his mother said as she reached down for the cane that she'd let fall to the floor earlier. "I want to show you something important."

"Well, let's go, then," Jake said as he reached an arm out to help his mother get to her feet. He was relieved it wasn't his father's inscription. "The dishes can wait while you show us."

"I just want it to be you," his mother said as she looked at him. "No one else. It's private."

Wade turned around to stare at that. Jake didn't blame him. They seldom talked about important things in their family, but when they did, they always did it out in the open where everyone could hear. Well, except for their secrets. Those they never talked about to anyone at any time.

"Don't worry about the dishes. We can get them," Cat said as she waved the two of them off.

"Yeah." Wade's voice was a little funny, although he rallied with a grin. "We'll want to have them done by the time Amy gets here. She's got enough on her mind without looking at our dirty dishes."

Jake nodded. "Thanks, then."

He hoped his mother didn't plan to show him her will or anything.

"Where do we need to go?" Jake asked as his mother took her first step.

"It's in my bedroom," she said as she took her second step.

"Could I bring it into the living room?" he asked. He was feeling a little curious now that she was making such a big deal about this.

"I've waited a long time for this day. You can wait a little longer," his mother said as she looked up and gave him a smile.

Jake was totally bewildered by her words. Then he figured she must be going to give him some remembrance of his father. A watch or something like that.

He couldn't imagine what that would be. The man's last watch had broken. His father went so few places he decided it was a waste of time to buy a new one when they had the clock in the kitchen that kept perfectly good time. Maybe his mother still had the old one and wanted him to get it repaired, though. Or maybe his father had something else.

As near as Jake could remember, the man hadn't owned any ties, so that was out. He had those pair of expensive cowboy boots, but they were almost worn out before he was killed and he thought Wade took them when he went off to the rodeo.

Jake gave up guessing when they were midway through the living room. Whatever it was, he'd pretend it was the best present anyone had ever received in the history of the world. And then he'd get it repaired as best he could and cherish it. Not because of his father, but because his mother had returned from prison and wanted her son to have something to remember his family by. He had to admire her determination to make the best of everything life threw at her.

Jake pushed open the door to the dark bedroom. Only the light from the door made it possible to see the shapes of the furniture inside.

His mother ran her hands against the wall next to the door until she found what she wanted.

"Here it is," she said as she flipped on the overhead light. Like in the kitchen, there was no light fixture. It was simply a bare bulb hanging down in the middle of the room showing everything up with a yellow glow.

"I could buy you some covers for the lights," he said as they started making their way to the bed. "Just let me know what you want and I'll have them delivered. Wade can get the ladder and put them up. Don't you try to do it, though. We can't have you falling again. Come to think of it, we should just get an electrician out and have the house rewired."

"I'm waiting to finish the kitchen before I do the lights," she said as she sat down on the bed.

"Well, I could help with both," Jake assured her as he sat down in the chair he'd used earlier. He could feel the wooden spindles across his back.

"You don't want to be wasting your money," his mother said as she reached over and patted his arm. She was sitting on the side of the bed right across from him on top of the same denim quilt he remembered being on the bed when he was a boy.

"Don't worry about the cost. I can…" He stopped. If he told her just how many electrical jobs and light fixtures he could buy for her, she wouldn't believe him. "I can get some secondhand globes really cheap and someone local can do the work."

"Once we've finished talking, you're going to need every penny you have saved," she said mysteriously. "I guarantee it."

"Okay," Jake said slowly. His mother didn't look upset. "If it's dad's watch, I can have it rebuilt inside. I'm sure there are places that do that kind of work."

She shook her head. "Now, why would we fix that old thing? He got it at some pawn shop in Billings. It wasn't worth anything when he bought it. It kept running longer than anyone expected. I don't even know where it is anymore."

"Okay," Jake repeated. He was officially out of clues.

"Bring me that picture sitting on the dresser," his mother said after some time had passed. "The small one in the brass frame at the back."

Jake stood up and walked over to the dresser. There had to be twenty framed photos sitting on the top of the thing, all well dusted and arranged neatly. Only one of them had a brass frame, though, so he picked it up and brought it back to his mother. He glanced at the photo when he first grabbed it, but he didn't get a good look because he didn't want to stare at it while his mother waited.

"Here." He held the picture out to her as he sat back in his chair. Suddenly, he thought he'd figured it out.

"You want me to find some old relative, is that it?" He'd always been told they had no aunts or uncles or cousins, but maybe there had been someone that no one ever talked about. A black sheep in the family. "A picture's not much to go on, but they have detectives now who can find anyone, even if they don't want to be found."

They had a lot of detectives like that looking for people in Las Vegas. Some of the investigators liked to play a little poker while they waited for their clues to come through. He couldn't imagine that anyone from either side of his parents' families could be that hard to find.

But his mother shook her head. "I think I already know where the relative is that I've discovered."

She handed the picture to him then.

"Well, that won't be hard, then," Jake said as he took it. "I'll just…"

He glanced down at the photo he held and everything stopped. It could have been a picture of Lara. The hair was shorter, of course, and not quite as curly, but the eyes had the same blue color and the hair was only slightly darker than hers. It was a boy, but he could have been her twin.

"That's your father when he was three," his mother said when he looked up at her in shock. "You boys all took after my side of the family, but your father had some German blood in him. His hair grew darker as he got older until it was more brown than blond."

Jake looked back at the photo. "I'll be.

Then he looked closer. "He doesn't appear to be very happy."

"It was his birthday," his mother continued. "And he didn't want to wear that little suit his mother had for him. She died the next year and that was the only picture he had of himself as a boy. His father wasn't much for family photos."

Jake handed the picture back. "So now you know."

His mother nodded. "I wasn't sure if you knew. That's why I wanted to tell you in private."

"I just found out before we left Las Vegas. Lara doesn't know and I don't think Cat has completely decided about whether to ever tell her." Jake's voice was bleaker than he had thought it would be. "Of course, it's probably for the best."

"How can that be for the best?" his mother asked indignantly. "Every child deserves to have a father."

Jake closed his eyes. "Sometimes kids wished they didn't have one, though."

It was so silent that Jake didn't open his eyes until seconds later.

"You're speaking of your father, of course," his mother said when he finally did. "I know he was an abusive man, but he was still your father."

"That's what worries me. There's that old saying that an apple doesn't fall far from the tree. Well, he's my tree."

"Oh, I see." His mother exhaled and he believed she really did understand. She put her hand on his arm in sympathy and he appreciated it.

They sat there together for a few more minutes.

"I still think it's worth taking a chance," his mother finally whispered. "You can choose to be the kind of man you want to be. With God's help, of course. I've seen people change when they turn to Him."

His heart broke when he saw her faith. She seemed to believe fiercely in what she said. He wasn't willing to gamble on it, though. He knew the odds. And God had never come through for him in the past.

"I'll talk to Cat about whether she can at least tell Lara that you're her grandmother," Jake finally said. "I know she'd be excited to know that much."

"I'll show Cat the photo, too, if you don't mind," his mother said. "There are people in Dry Creek who knew your father when he was a child. They might recognize his likeness in Lara's face. I don't want Cat to be caught by surprise if someone says something."

Jake nodded. "And everyone will be at the wedding tomorrow. Why don't you just stay sitting there and I'll go ask Cat to come in here? We might as well do it now."

He stood and walked toward the door. He didn't want to pressure Cat into doing anything she didn't want to do, but knowing how people in Dry Creek would all want to greet a little girl, he thought it was likely someone would spot her resemblance to the Stone family. He had not realized that his family's legacy would touch Lara whether he decided it should or not.

Cat looked over when Jake suddenly appeared in the doorway to the kitchen. She had a dishtowel in her hands and was drying a plate. "You're back."

She took a step closer to him, away from the counter.

Wade was running some more hot water into the sink to rinse the glasses they had used for supper. Lara had been assigned the task of wiping off the table with a wash rag. She was on her third pass by now, but it kept her busy, especially when she decided she needed to scrub the legs, too.

Everyone was busy with other things and Cat had the luxury of just looking at Jake. She wanted to remember him like this. His hair was deep black in the half shadow of the doorway and he wore a slight smile on his face. Emotion flared in his eyes as he stared back at her. The stubble on his cheeks was more pronounced than it had been this morning. His white shirt was wrinkled by now, but he had it open at the neck and, after feeling his gaze upon her, she wanted to go closer and press her face into the space under his chin where his skin was bare.

She turned to glance at Wade and assured herself he had his back to her and Jake. And Lara was still scrubbing.

Maybe she should go over to Jake, she told herself

as she turned back. Just to touch him so she could remember everything with enough clarity so she'd be able to wrap the moment around her when she was back in Minneapolis.

She stood there, tempted and undecided.

"I was wondering if you could come with me for a minute," Jake finally said, his low voice carrying softly across the space between them.

She blushed, even though there was no way he could have read her thoughts. She stepped back to set her dish towel on the counter before continuing the walk over to him. The living room behind Jake was in shadows.

She did not know what to say when she got near enough to reach out and touch him.

He held out his hand. "I wanted to show you something."

She smiled then and took his fingers. She felt his calluses as they slid smooth against the palm of her hand. With no further thought, she followed him into the darkness.

They were in the middle of the room when she squeezed his hand and he stopped. He turned toward her, but the only way she knew was because she suddenly felt her hands curled up against his chest. She hadn't realized how fine the cotton was that he wore, even though he'd been wearing the shirt since Las Vegas. Sometimes it took a touch to know the value of things, she thought, as she lifted her hand up to his face.

"I could be blind," she whispered as her fingers traced his face. "And I would still know you."

His jaw trembled as she ran her fingers over it.

And then, suddenly, his hands were holding her head, smoothing back her hair, and she knew he was going to kiss her.

His lips pressed against hers softly and then deepened until it filled every empty space in her heart. They were bound together for a moment. And then he moved to lean against her forehead, his breath coming hard.

As they stood there, she remembered then how often she had begged him to tell her stories of this house— and the lilacs. She'd dreamed of both. The lilacs were not in bloom, but they needed to kiss inside this place. His memories had been as close as she had come to having a home in her youth. In her mind, she always shared this place with him.

"I don't want to pressure you," he said finally, his voice rough.

She almost said she loved him, but she brought herself back from the brink. She didn't want to burden him with that when she might not have any future to offer him. And he had never made any declarations of love to her. He always said he would take care of her, but he never spoke of deeper feelings.

He found her hand again even though she'd dropped it to her side.

"Come," he said. "This is important."

She let him lead her to his mother's bedroom. The door was shut, but a strip of light showed around the bottom, and when he turned the knob and opened it, a soft light came out into the hallway.

Gracie was sitting on the bed and she looked up with a worried expression on her face. "Did you tell her?"

Jake shook his head. He had released her hand when

they walked into the room and he stood several feet away from her now. She supposed it was only natural. He wouldn't want his mother to think he was connected to her more strongly than friendship would warrant.

Finally, she realized he had the same frown on his face as his mother wore on hers.

"What is it?" she asked, wondering suddenly if they had heard about her medical condition.

His mother held out a small framed photograph that looked as if it had been sitting on her dresser for decades.

"I know." The woman gestured for Cat to take the photo.

"I don't understand," she said, but she took the photo anyway.

And then she looked down. The only light in the room came from the bare bulb almost directly over her head. At first she thought the glare on the glass was distorting the image, but she turned it slightly and saw that the photo didn't change that much.

"It's my father," Jake said as she kept staring at the picture. "The reason my mother wanted you to see it is because he was born in this house. There will be people around who will remember what he looked like at that age and they'll likely be at the wedding." He paused for a moment and then continued. "I know you wanted to spare Lara all of this. I don't know if there's a way to hide her face. Maybe get her a big hat. Or a scarf."

Cat felt the first tear trickle down her cheek before she even knew she was crying.

"It's my fault," Jake said as he stepped closer and put his arm around her shoulders. "I never should have brought you here until we had it worked out. I don't want you to feel forced into anything. It's your choice whether you tell her anything."

She shook her head as she leaned into his embrace. "It's not your fault. We sort of dropped at your feet from the sky. It just wasn't very good timing, I guess."

"I'm glad you came," Jake said, his voice sincere.

Gracie cleared her throat and Cat looked over at her. "The decision is yours, but I think a child deserves to know who her father is."

Cat was standing close enough to Jake that she could feel the ripple of tension move through him.

"And then what?" he said to his mother. "Lara might like me better as some distant uncle who sends her presents."

"You don't need to send things." Cat stepped away from him. "Lara and I will be all right. We do fine—just the two of us."

"You don't do fine," Jake said fiercely, turning from his mother to her. "And it's my responsibility to help you. You have my financial support regardless of what you tell Lara. But remember, she thinks her father is some fairy-tale prince off doing important things. I'm a two-bit gambler who's been lucky at the tables. There's no magic dust in my life. I don't want to fail her."

She and Jake were quiet for a few minutes and finally his mother stood up.

"You two need to talk," Gracie said as she reached for her cane. "And I'm going to go out and have some ice cream with my granddaughter."

"You can't—" Jake started, but his mother interrupted him.

"I'm not going to say anything," his mother promised as she started walking to the door. "Besides, if you do decide to tell her now, you need to be able to answer the one question she's sure to ask."

Cat looked up. "What's that?"

"When is Daddy going to marry Mommy?" Gracie stepped through the door into the hallway. She grinned as she reached back and shut the door behind her.

The question paralyzed Cat. She looked over at Jake. "I'm sorry. Lara won't really ask that. It will never even occur to her."

She went over and sat on the bed. "She won't expect anything."

Jake just stood there and suddenly he started to grin. "Oh, she'll expect a wedding, all right. I know that much about my girl. The prince always carries the princess away to his castle and they live happily ever after."

"She knows life isn't like that." Cat had the words out before she realized she was wrong. Her daughter did believe her life was a fairy tale. "Oh, dear."

Cat felt miserable. This was all getting complicated. "She'll understand that we can't get married."

"Really?" The smile was gone from Jake's face and his voice was curious.

Cat nodded. She could figure this out. She just needed to do it slowly. "No one should *have* to get married. That's not why I came to see you, anyway. I just need some time to tell Lara about you. She'll be fine."

"I see," Jake said. This time his voice had definitely flattened out.

She looked up at him, wondering why it was that

when her heart was breaking her tears had dried up. "We could still be friends, though."

He laughed, completely without humor. "Lara knows that the prince never just shakes hands and becomes friends with the princess. She's even got the kiss down. Ask her sometime."

With that, he walked out of the room, leaving the door partially open.

She'd set the photo down on the bed and she picked it back up again. She searched the man's face for some hint of the rage that had brought him down in his later years, but she saw none. His actions had left such deep hurts in the lives of others.

Lord, how long can I wait? You know what the doctor said. I don't have much time before the surgery. What if Jake never feels worthy of being a father? Am I wrong to wait to tell Lara until I'm sure?

She sat there for a few more minutes and then stood up and put the framed picture back on the dresser where it belonged. The man was dead; he shouldn't have so much power over his son. She listened and could hear laughter coming from the kitchen. She hoped Lara tucked the memory of this night deep inside her somewhere. She might need it in the years ahead.

She turned a little too quickly toward the door and felt a pain shoot through her. She had a hard time catching her breath and the room started to spin. She tried to step toward the bed, but a white mist seemed to overwhelm her. Her last thought as she sank to the floor was relief that she wasn't going to die with that photo in her hand. Jake would never forgive her for that, because he would have to explain it all to their daughter then.

Chapter Ten

Jake sat at the kitchen table. He was miserable, but was trying not to let it show. He knew Cat was disappointed in him, but a man needed to do what was right even if it made him unpopular. And, no matter which way he looked at it, he wasn't doing anyone any favors by pretending he could be a father. If he had the ability to change himself, that would be different. For a moment, he envied his mother and Cat their unblinking belief that God could do that for a man.

But they had the same look on their faces that he'd seen on tourists who wanted to play poker for the first time in Las Vegas. They thought they would get lucky and beat the pros. Some of the regulars called them "blind-bet pigeons," because they often couldn't even follow the speed of the other players and were easily plucked of all their money. Jake never sat down to a table with pigeons.

And he didn't want to lose the game now with Lara and Cat. He was best as an "uncle" and not a father.

Maybe if he didn't look in the mirror and see parts of his father in his own face it would be different. But there was something about the shape of his eyebrows and a fleeting glance he sometimes got when he saw his chin. His coloring all came from his mother, but his father was surely in him, as well.

Lara giggled and the pure joy of the sound brought him back from his brooding. She was sitting on the other side of the table with his mother next to her. Wade had brought out three cartons filled with ice cream— mango, vanilla and super-chunk chocolate—along with hot fudge and some things in little bottles. Right now, Lara was carefully placing pink things on top of her vanilla ice cream.

"How did you know to buy pink?" Jake asked his mother in surprise. She and Wade would never buy sprinkles for themselves. "Was that one of your, ah, impressions? The things you hear from God?"

"Of course not," she answered as she looked over at him, satisfaction evident in every line of her face. "Wade's the one who bought them."

Jake turned to arch an eyebrow at his older brother who was coming back to the table with a bottle of maraschino cherries. "Really? You and the pink stuff?"

His brother stopped in midstride and glared at him.

"You're blushing!" Jake realized in astonishment.

"They were for Amy, okay?" Wade growled as he finished walking to the table. He slammed the bottle of cherries down. "She likes pink."

Jake held up his hands in surrender. "Okay, I get it, then."

"No, you don't, but you would if you weren't too chicken to get married."

Jake figured there might be some humor in his brother's face, but it wasn't enough to make it better.

"My life is my business," Jake said curtly. "And it's fine."

He knew it was a lie when he said it. Nothing about his life had been fine since Cat walked into the hotel in Las Vegas. Not that it had been much more than adequate before that, but it was certainly stretching to call it fine now.

"Yeah?" Wade said as he sat down in the chair he'd used before. "You don't look like you're doing so good."

"Now, boys," his mother said, looking up from the pyramid of ice cream she was helping Lara decorate. "Let's be civil. We're having a party."

"Is it my birthday again?" Lara asked, excitement making her voice rise to a squeal. She had managed to find her plastic crown and put it on her head already so she was prepared.

"If you want it to be," his mother told the girl firmly and then looked over at him a little guiltily. "Kids don't get spoiled from having too many parties, do they?"

Jake shrugged. He certainly wasn't the one to reprimand anyone on that score. And he was happy to attend all of his daughter's birthday parties. He just wished Cat would come back to the kitchen so she could have some of the ice cream, too. She was still looking more peaked than he thought she should. Maybe some ice cream would make her feel better.

"Wade's right, you know," his mother leaned over and whispered to him a few minutes later while Lara was busy selecting a cherry from the jar and Wade had left the table to get a bigger spoon.

"People have to make their own decisions," he said.

His mother looked at him a moment. "They also need to take responsibility for their actions."

"I'm going to provide for them. I just haven't had a chance to meet with my accountant and ask him to send regular payments. But I'll do that when I get back to Las Vegas next week. They won't want for anything."

"Except you," his mother said and was quiet for a minute before finishing. "Your *friend,* Cat, is probably in my bedroom crying right now."

"Friendship is the best…" Jake started and then he realized all of what his mother had said. "You don't really think she's crying, do you? I thought she was just taking a few minutes to rest. She's tired. It was a long drive to get here and…" He stood. "I'm going to go check on her."

He didn't know what he would do if she was crying. He couldn't bear to have her unhappy. Maybe he just hadn't explained everything well enough. He was doing what was best for her and Lara by keeping his distance. That didn't mean he didn't love them.

The realization came to him so fast that he stopped halfway through the living room. It was dark except for the dim light shining out from the hall. He didn't know why it had taken him so long to realize that his worry about Cat was not all there was. He stood there and the only thing that ran through his mind was that loving them only meant he should do more to protect them.

Then he heard a moan and every muscle in his body went on alert. Cat wasn't sleeping and she was in pain. He could hear it in her voice. He forgot about walking and ran to the partially open door. At first all he could see was the bed and no one was lying there. He pushed the door completely open, though, and that's when he saw her. She was lying, crumpled on the floor by the dresser.

"Cat," he whispered as he went to her.

She didn't answer and her face was turned away from him so he couldn't see it. He bent down and leaned over to touch her cheek, hoping to wake her. Her skin was cold.

"Cat," he said again, moving his hands lightly over her scalp to see if she had fallen and hit her head on the dresser. Her hair fell between his fingers in silky strands, but he found no bumps or obvious cuts. Her breathing was shallow.

He'd taken a first-aid course at one of the casinos a year ago and he desperately tried to remember what else he should check for. He ruled out a drug overdose because he knew she would never take anything. Likewise with being drunk. Thinking back he remembered those were the two things the first-aid course had emphasized the most. He ran his hand down her back to be sure he hadn't overlooked a major break from a fall. The sweater she had worn since Las Vegas was thin enough that he saw there was nothing obvious in the way of broken bones. But he couldn't be sure without an X-ray.

And then he felt her stir. He had one hand on her back still and the other braced against the floor on the other side of her head, so when she turned, he was looking right down at her.

Her eyes opened and she stared at him for a moment.

"Do I get a kiss?" she whispered, a hint of mischief in her eyes.

"How can you joke about this?" Jake demanded and then he bent down and kissed her anyway.

Her lips were sweet.

When he pulled away, he didn't move back more than a couple of inches. He looked into her eyes and tried not to let his terror show. "Do you hurt anywhere? Did you fall? What happened?"

"I didn't break anything," she said, and then her eyes moved away from his.

She was hiding something.

"I know you're not fainting from hunger this time," he persisted. "And you say you're not pregnant. But something's wrong. I'm going to drive you into Miles City to the hospital."

This made her eyes lift back to his.

"But—" she started to say.

"I don't want you to worry. I'm paying for it, and Lara can stay here with my mom and Wade. She'll be fine. When was the last time you saw a doctor, anyway?"

She didn't answer for so long he thought she wasn't going to and then she said, "A week ago."

"Well, you're going to need a complete workup," Jake said as he leaned back on his heels. "Let me check you further to be sure you didn't break any bones in your fall. Then I'll lift you up to the bed."

"Mommy." The call sounded as if it was coming from the kitchen. "Come see my castle."

Cat reached up to touch his face and then she whispered, "Don't let Lara see me like this. I don't want to scare her."

Jake reached up and wrapped his hand around her fingers, before turning her palm so he could kiss the center of it. "I'll take care of everything. I'll lift you to the bed and then I'll go see Lara."

He didn't know what he'd say to the girl, but he'd do his best to reassure her that nothing was wrong with her mother.

"You're sure nothing feels like it's broken?" he asked as he squatted down and moved so his arms were under her legs and back.

"I'm fine, just…" Cat said.

"Put your arms around my neck," he said.

When she had done so, he lifted her, straightening his knees slowly as he stood.

"There," he said softly as he turned and laid her on the bed.

When he had her settled, he sat down on the edge of the bed and took her hand. "I don't want you to worry, either. The doctors will find out what's wrong. It will be okay."

She smiled at him then, a little sadly. "When you get back, we need to talk."

"Mommy," Lara called again from the kitchen. "My castle is melting."

Jake stood up. "I'll go see to her and ask Wade to go out and start the engine on my pickup so the cab can warm up before I take you out. It's cold tonight."

"I really don't need to go," Cat protested.

"Yes," Jake said as he turned back on his way to the door. "Yes, you do.

"I'll be back in a minute," he said and with that he stepped through the door.

Cat watched him leave the room. Maybe she did need to have a doctor look at her again. She knew all about the congenital defect in her heart, but maybe it had gotten worse. She hadn't been fainting like this before. If her heart was deteriorating, she didn't have much time. She'd talk to the doctor and then tell Jake she wanted him to be Lara's guardian if something happened. There was no more time for him to adjust to being a father. The doctor would surely tell her she needed to get back to Minneapolis right after the wedding and have surgery.

She looked at the ceiling of the room. Gracie and her husband must have lain here and stared up at this same ceiling when they had troubles. Jake had told him that he and both of his brothers had been born in this bed. She liked the sense of family she had in this room, from the photos on the dresser to the old white-cotton bathrobe that hung on a hook just outside the closet.

Jake had told her once that the people in Dry Creek bought their bathrobes with an eye to their later use as costumes in the Christmas pageant. White was for the angels. It was such a lovely tradition, she thought as her eyes almost closed.

She heard footsteps hurrying through the living room and forced her eyes to remain open. Finally, she saw Jake appear again in the doorway to the bedroom.

"I told Lara that you and I are going to take a drive,"

he announced as he came inside. "And I took Wade aside to explain everything and he's going to turn the heater on in the pickup. Then he'll call Amy and the two of them will follow us into Miles City."

Cat tried to pull herself up. "Oh, not on the night before their wedding. They shouldn't have to do that."

"Wade won't stay back," Jake said, coming over to the bed. "He's my brother and I'd have to tie him down to make him sit this out. He knows I'd do the same for him."

"Well, at least tell Amy she doesn't need to come," Cat said as she put her arms around Jake's neck again. "She must have all those last-minute things to do."

Jake wrapped the quilt she'd been lying on around her. "Amy won't hear of it, either."

"My purse," she whispered. She'd need her insurance card and maybe the phone number of her doctor back in Minneapolis.

Jake set her purse on top of her. Then he put his arms under her and lifted her up. "We'll need to keep you warm."

He left the light on as he walked out of the bedroom. She liked being held close like this as he walked easily through the living room.

"Did you tell your mom?" Cat finally remembered. She felt drowsy. "So she'll know Lara's staying with her."

"She overheard enough of what I told Wade," he said.

It took all of Cat's concentration just to hang on to her consciousness. The door was still open as they walked into the kitchen.

Cat turned her head and saw her daughter with a spoonful of ice cream in her hand.

"I'm eating my castle," Lara said proudly. "If I don't, it will melt."

Lara had no sooner finished talking that she started to stare at Cat.

"Everything's fine, pumpkin," Cat said. "I'm going to be gone for a little while, but you stay here with Jake's mother and be a good girl."

Lara looked as though she was on the verge of tears.

"I love you," Cat said, tears of her own coming too close. "Just get a good night's sleep and remember, tomorrow is the wedding."

Lara's face didn't clear at the promise of that.

"There will be cake," Jake said as he carried her past the table. "Big pieces of cake."

That finally made Lara smile. "Like my birthday cake?"

"You'll have to wait and see," Cat said as they went through the door.

"Oh," she breathed out as Jake kicked the door shut behind them. The night was black and, if it wasn't for the headlights on Wade's pickup, Jake wouldn't be able to see the ground well enough to walk safely.

Wade wasn't in his pickup, but was waiting beside the passenger door of Jake's vehicle. He opened the door as they arrived and Jake slid her into her place in the cab and then tucked the quilt around her.

Jake closed the door and walked around to the driver's side. He climbed in and put the key in the ignition. "Wade's going to stop and pick up Amy and meet us at the hospital. We won't wait for them."

Cat nodded. It was too much effort to speak.

The beams of the headlights followed the gravel road as Jake drove steadily. He didn't try to talk to her, but she noticed he kept glancing over at her. The inside of the cab was dark, but Wade was following them down the road and the lights from his pickup showed her Jake's face. He was worried, a small frown settling on his forehead. He'd put a jacket on and the collar was turned up around his neck. He'd sat his hat on the seat between them, but she wondered if he wore it at night. He'd never had a Stetson back in the home. There was so much she wanted to learn about him.

She set her hand down on the seat between the two of them and he reached down to hold it.

She felt better being connected to him.

"If something happens to me," she managed to whisper, "will you take care of Lara?"

"Of course," he said, too quick and certain. She knew he didn't understand all that she was asking of him, but she was suddenly too tired to continue. The hospital would have something to revive her. She'd talk to Jake then. In the meantime, the only one she had the energy to converse with was God.

Lord, she began wordlessly. *You know my need. Be with me tonight.*

Chapter Eleven

Thanks to a call from his mother to Mrs. Hargrove, the hospital was expecting Cat when Jake brought her in. His mother hadn't known who to call, but she knew her friend would. Jake parked in front of the main door and two men in white uniforms rushed out with a gurney. They pulled it close to the passenger door and had Cat out of the cab and were strapping her onto the gurney when Jake got around to the other side. They were ready to head back inside and Jake ran to press the door open for them.

Fluorescent lights filled the inside of the building with a white glare. Jake could hear the wheels of the gurney as the staff took Cat down the left hallway. He started in that direction when someone called him back.

"You need to fill out the forms first, sir," a woman from behind a counter said.

"Just let me see that she's settled."

"She'll be back out in the waiting room in a heartbeat if she doesn't have any forms," the woman said. "Trust me. You don't want that."

Jake turned around and walked over. "I thought Mrs. Hargrove called."

"She did."

"Is it about payment, then?" He pulled out his credit card and laid it on the counter. "This will cover it."

He had a high limit. Very high.

"We also need her name," the woman said, without touching the card. "No one told us that."

"Cat— I mean, Cathy Barker."

The woman wrote that down. "Address?"

"Minneapolis," Jake said.

The woman looked up from the form and arched her eyebrow. "Minneapolis is a big place. Can you be more specific?"

"I don't know the address," Jake admitted in defeat.

The woman thought for a moment. "So you're not married? To each other, I mean."

"No." He snapped out the words and then took a deep breath. "But we should be."

He looked sideways at the woman, embarrassed he'd revealed that much. "I mean—well—just put Dry Creek down for her address. The Stone Ranch."

The woman smiled. "Mrs. Hargrove told me about your family."

"Then you know I'm good for the charges," Jake said in relief.

"I don't know about that. She never said anything about you boys all having money. I mean, I know your brother Wade won lots of rodeo prize money over the years. I've seen his picture in the paper. But aren't you the gambler?"

"I'm very good at what I do even if I don't have my picture in the paper."

The woman studied him skeptically.

He picked up his credit card and handed it to her. "Go ahead and put a hold on this for fifty thousand dollars. That should be enough for tonight, won't it? We can settle up in the morning."

The woman took the card and gave him one last look. "You could be bluffing. That's what gamblers do."

"Just run the card." He heard his teeth grinding.

The woman smiled. "You should get married, you know. Feeling the way you do."

Jake told himself only a fool took advice on his love life from someone he didn't even know. "I asked her once and she didn't talk to me for almost five years."

"Well," the woman said. "Have you tried flowers?"

"She likes lilacs," he admitted.

"So hang around for a couple of months. We'll have lilacs all around the hospital by then. You can pick her a few."

Jake saw a flash of headlights drive by the front entrance going toward the parking lot. "That will be my brother, Wade. He'll vouch for me. So, can I just go see how she is?"

The woman studied him some more and then she picked up the phone. "I have a visitor for the woman you just brought in. Where should he go?"

She hung up the phone. "One of the orderlies will come and get you in a minute. Just wait over there by the door."

She pointed to the end of the hall where Cat had been taken.

By the time he got to the meeting place, one of the men who'd wheeled Cat inside was there.

"You can see her in a few minutes," he said. "The emergency room staff is still doing an assessment and getting her stabilized."

"But she's okay?"

"I can't really say," the man began stiffly and loosened up. "But we have a real good team in emergency tonight. They'll know something soon. In the meantime, you can wait in this room here."

The man swung a door open and led Jake into a small waiting room. There were a dozen chairs lined against the walls and a television in a corner. A table on one side held some magazines.

"I'll come get you the minute we're done," the orderly said and then turned to leave.

Jake sat down. "Could you send word out to my brother that I'm back here? He'll be coming through the main door with his fiancée any minute. Name's Wade Stone."

"The rodeo star?" the orderly looked back to ask, sudden interest in his voice.

"That's the one." Jake stood up again. He knew an opening when he saw one. "If you bring me some news about the woman you just brought in, I could get you an autograph from him."

"Really?"

"Sure."

"All I need is an authorization to give you information," the orderly said as he turned completely around and held out his hand to Jake. "Proof that you're her husband. A driver's license will do."

"Oh."

"Ah." The orderly pulled his hand back. "Sorry. Hospital rules, you know. You can be a visitor, but I can't release any information unless you're related. Privacy violation. She might not want you to know something."

The man left and Jake eased back down in the chair. When had hospitals become so concerned with who was married to who? He might understand it in the maternity ward, but this was the regular emergency room. Weren't they just supposed to worry about healing people here?

The door opened then and Wade rushed in with his fiancée, Amy, at his side.

Jake stood up.

Amy, her blond hair clipped back, was as fresh faced and beautiful as he remembered from his boyhood. She used to hang out with him and Wade whenever they let her. He'd been a little put out when Wade told him they were engaged. He'd never noticed any romance blooming between the two of them when they were kids. Maybe he didn't know as much about women and romance as a man should.

"We got here as fast as we could," Amy said as she hurried over and gave him a hug. "I feel terrible now that I didn't come over earlier and say hello. And now your friend is in the hospital."

Amy released him and Wade stepped up.

"What do the doctors say? How is she?" his brother asked as he reached over and gave Jake a pat on the shoulder.

"They won't tell me anything because I'm not married to her."

"Oh." His brother grimaced.

"You'd think it would count for something that we had a baby together," Jake muttered, forgetting where he was and who he was talking to.

"What?" Wade asked in amazement. "I thought you said she wasn't pregnant."

"Not now," Jake said, realizing he had given away too much not to tell all of it. "It's Lara."

"Lara! Sweet Lara!" his brother echoed in delight as he thumped Jake on the back again. "She's your daughter!"

Jake nodded, a grin on his face. "And Cat will be upset with me for saying anything. She hasn't told Lara yet."

"We're going to have another party!" Wade insisted. "And don't worry. The nurse at the desk said she thinks Cat will be just fine."

"Did she say anything more?" Jake asked eagerly. "What's wrong with her, anyway?"

"Well, she only saw Cat briefly when they brought her in, but she said they usually call for backup by now if anything serious is wrong."

Just then Jake heard a flurry of activity out in the hall and he headed for the noise. That sounded like backup to him. He needed to get some answers.

Cat felt better since they'd started giving her oxygen. She was lying on a hospital bed with green curtains drawn all around her. Her clothes were on the table at the foot of the bed and she had a cotton gown tied around her with tiny blue squares on it. She was hooked up to more machines than she'd ever seen in her life.

But, at least, she didn't feel as if she was going to faint any longer. She even smelled the odor of sharply scented cleaning products so she knew she was in a well-kept facility.

The doctor pulled the curtains back and stepped inside. "I reached your doctor in Minneapolis. He explained everything. And he said to tell you that you shouldn't be running around the country. Your heart needs to be in better shape for surgery."

The man was pleasantly rumpled and balding. He scowled a little as he talked, though. "And I happen to agree with him. I said it would be another day at the earliest before we can start transporting you to Minneapolis for the surgery."

"I thought I had more time," she said. "I guess I should change my airline tickets now, though. My daughter and I are scheduled to fly back out of Las Vegas, but we will have to leave from somewhere else."

The doctor grabbed the chart that hung on the end of her hospital bed and lifted it up to make some notes.

"Billings is the closest airport from here," he said when he finished. "There should be a direct flight in from Minneapolis most days."

She nodded. Last-minute changes like that usually meant higher charges. Fortunately, she had some savings.

He hesitated. "I don't think flying in a commercial airplane will be the answer, though. You wouldn't be able to stay on your oxygen, and any change in cabin pressure is hard on hearts."

"Maybe I could rent a car."

"Absolutely not. You're likely to pass out at any time. You shouldn't be driving."

They were both silent for a minute. Muffled footsteps went by the bed, but no one looked in. There were snippets of conversations all around them. Cat wondered how much other misery there was in this place tonight.

"Your doctor there said you were worried about establishing a guardian for your daughter before you had the surgery."

"Yes."

The man looked tired. "Well, I can understand you making the trip out here, then. It's just that it couldn't have come at a worse time."

"It was the only time." She felt suddenly chilled and moved the sheet higher up around her chin.

His eyes filled with sympathy. "And have you been successful in finding someone?"

"Not as much as I had hoped."

"Ah."

She felt a tear start to form and she reached up to wipe it away. "Her father will support her financially, but he doesn't want to be a hands-on kind of parent. Maybe he'll send her to a school or something."

The desolation was clear in her voice, but she didn't have the strength to hide it.

"Ah," the doctor said again.

"That's better than foster care, isn't it?"

He glanced down for a moment before looking back up and, by the time he did, his smile was forced. "Well, we're going to have to put that worry aside for the time being. You should avoid any stress in the next day or so. Your heart needs to rest the best it can."

"I didn't mean to make it worse," Cat whispered. "Did I? Make it much worse?"

She was confessing and hoping for redemption at the same time.

The doctor hesitated, but at least his gaze was steady. "It's always a delicate surgery. If you rest, you might almost have as good of a chance of pulling through as you had a week ago."

"Sixty percent still?"

"I don't want you to worry. The percentage doctors give is just our way of warning people to be careful."

"How much has it gone down?"

He didn't answer at first and then he spoke. "A few points. That's why we want to build you up before you go back."

"I'll do everything you tell me to do," Cat pledged. She had gotten Lara this far; she wanted to stay beside her the whole way. If she did that, she wouldn't need to worry about what Jake would do if he became the sole guardian.

The doctor glanced over at the machines that were monitoring her. "Everything looks like it should." He smiled as he looked down. "Get some sleep if you can. The orderlies will be by before too long to take you to a regular room."

He pulled the curtains shut again as he left and Cat felt her eyes close.

Dear Lord, she began and didn't even know how to pray so she just ended it with, *Have mercy on me, Dear Lord.*

She did not know how long she had lain there, trying to sleep, when she heard a movement. She thought it was just a nurse checking her vitals so she didn't open her eyes.

"Cat."

She barely heard the whisper, it was so soft. She knew the voice, though, and looked up. Jake was standing at the foot of the bed, looking as out of place as she had ever seen him. Maybe it was the intense look in his eyes. He usually had a confident attitude, but he looked thoroughly subdued. The light was low in the curtained area and his face was halfway in shadows.

"Are you okay?" he whispered. "They won't tell me anything."

"I'm just supposed to rest," she assured him. "I need to have heart surgery." She saw his body jerk at that news, but she kept on talking. "I've needed to have it for some time now. Apparently, I was born with a defect in my heart. It didn't bother me much until recently, although it's been around."

"When you fainted at the home?"

She nodded. "They didn't know what the problem was, but yes."

"I should have made you go to a doctor back then."

"You're not God," she snapped at him then. "You don't have to fix everything."

He was surprised and she was tired.

"Sorry," she mumbled and continued, "I'll need to go back to Minneapolis pretty soon so my doctor there can do surgery to fix it."

She was too weary to explain more about everything. "I shouldn't have said what I did about you being God."

"Well, I'm not, you know," he said softly.

She smiled at that, and when she looked up at him, she knew that was what he'd intended her to do.

It was silent for a moment and she heard the sound of him walking around to the side of her bed. He wore his boots, but he stepped lightly.

Jake reached out and caressed her cheek. "We're going to do everything we need to make that surgery a success."

Jake moved his hand from her face and curled it around her fingers. He took a breath as he did so, and it was as though he commanded her to breathe, too.

"We're going to make it," he said, and then he inhaled again.

Cat felt herself breathe with him.

Without loosening the bond between their hands, Jake looked over his shoulder and pulled the chair along the wall close. Then he settled himself in it.

"I need to be the one to tell Lara who you are," Cat whispered. "She won't believe anyone else."

Jake nodded. "I'll have someone bring her in."

They sat there together, not talking. They were breathing together. Jake would periodically move up and gently brush her hair back with his other hand and once he stroked the inside of her palm.

"First thing in the morning," Cat finally roused enough to say. "I need to be sure and tell her."

Jake's breath caught and she looked at him. She decided it must be growing darker in the room. She thought she saw a tear run down his cheek, but that couldn't be right. Jake didn't cry.

"Promise me," she whispered anyway. "Don't let anything happen until I tell Lara."

He nodded. "I promise. Hush, now. Everything will be fine."

And he took another deep breath and she followed him.

"Tell me a story," she murmured after a while, "from when you were a boy."

"The crops were late one year," he started. "The spring wheat not rising much higher than the tops of those old boots I was wearing. But I was out trying to cut down on the grasshoppers day after day. We knew they'd eat more than we'd harvest if we didn't do something. They were all over the place, jumping and eating their fill. It was Wade that came up with the idea of sprinkling pepper on them. He'd heard it worked on some kind of a bug. He couldn't remember which one, but we figured it was worth trying. So we hauled out every pepper shaker we could find in the kitchen and threw the stuff all around."

"What happened with the pepper? Did it kill the grasshoppers?"

He smiled. "Turned out they liked their wheat with pepper and just kept eating. All that happened was that mom was spitting mad at us. We didn't have any pepper on our fried eggs for a month. I never did find out what kind of bug doesn't like pepper."

"You boys, you worked hard."

Jake nodded and reached up to smooth the hair away from her face.

"You're beautiful," he whispered then. "Did I ever tell you that?"

Then he bent down and kissed her on the forehead.

She smiled. "I wish I could see the lilacs blooming on your ranch. Just once."

"I'll bring you back in a couple of months and you can smell your fill of their fragrance."

Cat closed her eyes. It wouldn't hurt to take a little nap. Jake was here. He'd take care of anything that happened.

"Remember to come back in the morning," she muttered.

"I'm not leaving," he whispered as his fingers caressed her cheek again.

It was so nice to feel his hands on her face, she thought to herself.

"We need to get married," Jake said.

Her whole body jumped.

"Keep breathing," he said. "It doesn't need to be scary. I just need to have some claim on Lara if— I mean, we both know the state well enough to know they won't give custody of a little girl to a man who isn't related to her."

"Oh," Cat said. Of course, he was right.

"Breathe," Jake commanded and she did. Her heartbeat was settling down.

"I didn't think of that. Maybe it could just be until— well, I mean, if I live, we wouldn't need to stay that way."

"You're going to live," he said, determination in his voice.

"Maybe you and she could do a paternity test instead," she murmured and she could hear her voice fading. "Then you wouldn't need to…"

Suddenly, she forgot what she meant to say. It was too much energy to speak anyway. She was so very tired and Jake was here. They'd talk tomorrow.

She turned her cheek toward him as his hand stroked her face and that was the last thing she did before sleep came.

Chapter Twelve

Jake woke with a start. A shaft of early-morning light was coming in through the gap in the curtains that hung high on the window. He'd fallen asleep with his head on Cat's bed and he still sat on the metal folding chair next to it. A beeping was coming from somewhere and he saw a red light flashing.

He squinted. Between the faint light from outside and the red light from inside, he could barely make out Cat's face. She looked pink. But when he reached out and touched her, she was cold. And she didn't move.

Just as he realized something was wrong, the night nurse came rushing in, leaving the door open so light flooded in from the hall. Then he could see Cat's skin wasn't rosy at all. It was pale as white marble and had a blue hue to it.

"What's going on?" he asked softly so he wouldn't disturb Cat, but the nurse didn't answer him.

Instead, she looked at the buttons on the machine next to the bed and pushed another one on the bed. Then there was a pulsing sound calling some kind of a code out in the hallway.

The woman looked at him as though she had just realized he was still there. "Move away from the bed."

He stood up and stepped back, sliding the chair back with him so it was out of the way, as well.

The nurse was on the bed now, straddling Cat and pressing her hands against his friend's chest to keep her heart beating. Seconds later another woman came in and then they were joined by the doctor Jake had seen last night walking around the emergency room.

"Clear the room of visitors," the doctor commanded with a stern look at Jake. "Wait outside."

"I can't," Jake whispered, but no one paid him any more attention. He gripped the rim of the chair without wondering why. He'd been holding it and he was paralyzed. Cat couldn't die, could she?

He watched the medical team at work. *Lord,* he whispered without thinking, *You can't be that cruel. Not to me. Not to Lara. Please, not this.*

He hadn't wrestled with God like this since his mother was on trial. He had brought all his fury against Him to argue for his mother and he hadn't been successful. He didn't have that kind of rage in him now. Losing Cat would break him until there would be no room for anger. There would just be nothing. How did a man stand against something like this? Cat's body was shutting down and he couldn't make the blood flow for her. He was helpless.

Finally, the pounding and the rushing stopped. It was quiet finally. The lights on the monitors flickered, but there were no alarms going off.

The doctor stepped back. "Give her some room now."

The nurses moved away from the bed, one of them stopping to smooth the sheet over Cat before she did.

"Is she okay?" Jake asked softly. His throat felt hoarse, as though he'd been holding his breath.

The doctor turned. "I thought you were supposed to leave last night." Then he shrugged. "I guess it's too late for that now. We're not supposed to give any information out to nonfamily members, you know."

"I'm her fiancée." Jake offered up the only bargaining chip he had.

The doctor raised his eyebrow in skepticism. "That's not the way I heard it when I talked to her earlier."

"I asked her to marry me last night. And she agreed."

It had not been an enthusiastic acceptance of his proposal. In fact, he wasn't sure she hadn't reversed her initial decision, but Jake figured the doctor did not need to know everything.

As it was, the man seemed to know enough. "I suppose she figured you'd be more likely to stay around for your daughter if she said yes."

Jake was silent.

The doctor didn't speak for a bit and then he gave Jake one long look. "Here's the deal. It's not good. Her heart stopped for a bit there. It's not pumping blood like it should, even with the rest and the oxygen. If she was in Minneapolis, we'd be rushing her into the surgery room. But we're a small hospital. More of a clinic than anything. We don't have the staff or the equipment to take on that kind of heart surgery here."

"We need to get her to Minneapolis then," Jake reasoned. "Right away."

The doctor paused and whispered, "She'd never make it."

At first, Jake thought he hadn't heard the man right.

The last of the two nurses left the room then, and Jake was still standing there, trying to convince himself the doctor hadn't given up.

"She'll just have to get better right here, then, until she's well enough to make the trip to Minneapolis?" Jake finally said.

The doctor didn't meet his eyes.

"Well, we can't just let her die!"

"We're doing all we can."

"That's not good enough," Jake said, determination building inside him as he spoke. "There has to be a way to do this. We can get one of those medevac helicopters you hear about to fly her over."

"That's what I was thinking of when I said she might not make it," the doctor answered slowly and then looked Jake squarely in the eyes. "It's risky to take her up with her heart in the condition it's in. I tried to convince her doctor to fly here and do the surgery, but he has commitments in Minneapolis."

"What kind of commitments?" Jake asked, his voice indignant. This couldn't be happening.

He glanced back at Cat and saw that the color in her face looked better. What could be more important in any doctor's schedule than saving a life?

"He's a speaker tonight at some kind of fundraiser for the hospital. They're trying to raise money for kids without insurance who need surgeries. He feels passionate about it. Knows some of the kids it would help.

He says they need the money now or it will be too late for a couple of them."

The man's voice trailed off. "He wouldn't be able to get a flight into Billings today, anyway. The early-morning one already left Minneapolis and the ones with stops won't get in until this evening."

Jake felt resolve grow out of the despair inside him. He wasn't going to just shake his fist at the heavens over this. He was going to win this battle, with or without God's help.

"What is his fundraising goal?" Jake's voice was strong and calm now that he knew what to do. He'd had good fortune at the poker tables, but he'd made sound investments with his winnings, too.

The sun was shining into the room better now. A new day was beginning.

"I think he mentioned a half million dollars. I know it's not much in medical terms, but he waives his fees so it's only the hospital bill that's left. I think he said there are five kids, illegal aliens all of them, who will live because of the money he raises tonight. Some kind of government aid might be possible, but it's not certain at this point."

"Call and tell him I'll send him his half million dollars and add another hundred thousand to the pot if he gets on a plane and does the surgery here. The folks at the fundraiser can entertain themselves or, if he wants, I can fly in one of the best comedians in Las Vegas to keep them happy."

The doctor lifted his eyebrow again. "That's right, you're the gambler. Mary at the reception desk told me. Said she's been afraid to run your credit card so it's still just sitting on her desk. The poor woman has a soft heart."

"Tell her it's good." Jake glared at the doctor. "I don't lie. And, after Mary runs that card, tell your doctor friend that the odds don't get any better than this. He wins no matter what. And I know someone who'll help me arrange for a private plane to fly him here."

"Gamblers bluff," the doctor said with a shrug to his shoulders. His eyes looked as if he wanted to believe, but he just shook his head.

"I'll let you talk to my banker." Jake pulled out his cell phone.

"There's no coverage here," the doctor replied, the hope that had flickered briefly in his eyes died. "But you probably knew that."

"Try me," Jake demanded. "There has to be a land-line around here that I can use."

Jake looked over at Cat. She seemed to be breathing regularly again. "The nurses will look in on her while we go use a phone, won't they?"

The doctor nodded. "I need to go back to my office now, anyway. You can use the phone there."

"And Cat?"

"I'll have someone come and sit with her."

Jake looked at the man. "Let's go then. But if she wakes up, I want the nurse to tell her I'm coming right back."

The doctor smiled slightly. "I think they can manage that."

When they stepped out of the room, Jake almost stopped. He didn't remember the hallways being this short. The building was three stories tall, but it really wasn't much more than a clinic. "You do have operating rooms here?"

The other man nodded. "The doctor from Minneapolis might need to fly in some equipment, but we should have enough of most things to do the surgery. It's not ideal, of course. But he goes all over the world. Surgeons operate in war zones and African countries with less than we have here."

"War zones?" That did halt Jake.

The fluorescent light in the hallway, above him, was flickering. He hadn't seen those kinds of lights used in decades. He looked around. The paint was chipped in places. A couple of worn wheelchairs were gathered at the end of the hall. This place was not prosperous. He wondered just how close to a war zone it came.

"Tell the doctor to bring what he needs with him. I'll get another plane if there's not enough room in the one plane for all of it."

A few minutes later, they were standing at the counter in front of Mary. She didn't smile at Jake and he figured that was not an encouraging sign. He wondered briefly how she could have been working last night and still be on duty this morning. Then he realized it hadn't been that many hours ago since he and Cat walked through the hospital doors for the first time. It probably wasn't even six o'clock in the morning now. He tried to remember if he had heard the rattle of breakfast trays going down the hall to the rooms, but he couldn't.

"Go ahead and run this guy's credit card," the doctor instructed the clerk while looking over at Jake. "Let's see what he's made of."

"How much should I…" Mary stopped to bite her lower lip in confusion.

"Might as well run it for the full fifty thousand limit the card takes for one transaction," Jake said. "We'll be paying that before the day is over if things go my way."

The doctor nodded.

The woman looked hesitant, but she picked up the card and punched some numbers into a machine. Then she positioned the card, ready to swipe it. Then she closed her eyes and ran the card through with one fluid motion of her hand.

A receipt started printing.

"Did it work?" the doctor asked.

Mary ripped off the receipt and peered closely at the numbers. Then she nodded without speaking and handed the receipt to Jake. "You'll need to sign on the line."

"Thank the Lord," the doctor said, a grin splitting his face as he turned to Jake and extended his hand. "I confess I didn't believe you were telling us the truth, but it appears you might be."

"I am," Jake replied, shaking the hand. "But I wouldn't be thanking God too much just yet."

The doctor looked at him, his face a question.

"Money's nothing," Jake said. "If God is going to give us a blessing, I want it to be on that operating table."

The other man nodded. "Next stop is my office. You can use the phone in there to call whoever you need. I wouldn't even know who to call to arrange some of the stuff we'll need."

Jake grinned for the first time. "The good thing

about playing poker with high rollers is that they tend to be the movers and the shakers. There's not much we could need that I wouldn't know someone to ask how to get it." He stopped and then from somewhere inside him came the words. "Except for prayer, maybe. Not many religious people at the big-stake tables in Las Vegas."

"Oh," the receptionist said and turned pink when Jake turned to look at her.

"I just called Mrs. Hargrove a few minutes ago," she said. "My shift is ending soon and I wanted to be sure they put your friend on the prayer chain in the Dry Creek Church. I didn't mention any names or anything, not even what was wrong, but…" Her voice trailed off.

"Thank you," Jake whispered. "You mean well."

That wasn't much of a ringing endorsement and he could see by the expression in her eyes that she realized that, too. But he didn't have time to explain that he hadn't given any thought to the words he'd spoken about needing God's help. He was sleep deprived and not himself. The truth was, he didn't expect any help to be coming no matter what anyone prayed. Jake and the doctors were on their own.

The doctor was already walking down the hall and Jake needed to follow him.

Suddenly, the doctor stopped and turned around.

Mary looked up at him.

"Call the lab and have them set up a place for people to donate blood. I don't know how much we'll need for the Barker surgery, but we don't want to be low."

Then the doctor glanced at Jake as he started walking again. "I'm assuming you'll give blood. We're going to need type O positive, but the Red Cross will credit us with donations and switch out some of what we have for what the Barker woman will need."

Jake nodded as he started to roll up the sleeve on his shirt. "I'll be ready to go after we make our phone calls."

They walked silently.

"Will they let me give twice?" Jake asked.

The doctor stopped walking and looked at Jake. "She's got you scared, does she?"

Jake nodded.

"Good," the doctor said, and called back down the hall to Mary, "Get in some cookies and juice for the blood donors. It's going to be a long day."

"I'm assuming you'll bring in the friends and family," the doctor added to Jake as he opened the door to a small room.

"Me?" Jake stopped in astonishment. He'd give Cat every drop of blood he had in him, but he didn't know how to ask many others. Wade would probably give. And his mother might, although he didn't know if she was eligible. Maybe Amy would do it, too. "Would three donors be enough?"

"Not even close," the doctor said as he walked into the room and pointed at the black telephone on the desk. "But let's worry about the doctor first. Go ahead and sit. You have some phoning to do."

Jake nodded. One step at a time. That's how he would make this happen. If he could just keep breathing.

Cat dragged the air into her lungs. She wasn't doing well and she knew it. Each in and out of her breath felt as if it was too much work. The sun was starting to come inside the hospital room. She had seen the same nurse sitting beside her bed, reading something, each time she floated up to consciousness. Cat realized she could die. Then she decided, if this was to be her last day, she didn't want to spend it in darkness.

"Curtains," she whispered and the nurse set down her journal and leaned closer.

"Please open," Cat added.

The nurse stood up and nodded. Then she walked over and pulled the curtains apart so the room was filled with sunshine.

"Better," Cat murmured.

The effort of it all had made her tired. She told herself that's why she didn't ask where Jake had gone. She was out of energy. She knew that wasn't the real reason, though. She couldn't bear to face the fact that he had left. She tried not to blame him. No one liked to stay in hospitals. She was grateful he'd waited to leave until she'd gone to sleep last night.

And then she looked up and he was standing in the doorway. His hair was rumpled and his shirtsleeves rolled up. There were circles around his eyes she hadn't noticed before, but when he saw her looking up at him, he smiled.

She forgot to breathe and it had nothing to do with the poor condition of her heart.

"Hi," she whispered.

He stepped inside then and walked quickly up to the side of her bed. The nurse who had been sitting in the chair stood up and started walking toward the door. Jake sat down in the chair the woman vacated and reached out a hand so he could entwine his fingers with Cat's as they lay on top of the quilt.

"You're going to be all right," he said then, and the satisfaction in his voice eased the fear inside her chest.

"When are they going to let me go to Minneapolis?"

"Your surgeon is coming here. All you need to worry about is getting yourself ready for surgery."

She frowned and tried to sit up. "But my insurance company has it set up in Minneapolis."

"Your surgeon has talked to them. It's all taken care of. All you need to do is keep breathing, as deep as you can to get the air in your lungs."

She found herself breathing in rhythm with him again. It was as though he carried her along with his strength.

"I need to tell Lara," she whispered after a few minutes. "I need to be the one to tell her that you are her father."

Jake nodded. "I'll ask my brother to bring her in for a few minutes. The wedding isn't until this afternoon."

"Oh, the wedding." Cat sighed. "I had forgotten."

She touched the edge of his shirt. "I hope you have another one to wear to the wedding. This one needs a good pressing."

"I'm not going to the wedding," Jake said calmly. "I'm going to stay with you. Wade's going to ask Charley Nelson to be his best man in my place."

"Oh, you can't do that," she said. "He's your brother. I'll be fine by myself for a few hours."

Suddenly she noticed the white bandage on his wrist. "What happened?"

"I gave blood for your surgery," he answered. "And don't worry. Wade understands."

Cat nodded. She didn't have the strength to argue. Everything felt so light, as though it wasn't important, anyway. She didn't understand how the surgery could be done here, but she was going to float on the knowledge. She needed to save what presence of mind she had now for her talk with Lara.

She wondered if someone had drawn the curtains again. The light in the room seemed to be fading away. Even though she had her eyes closed, she sensed the light was leaving. From somewhere, she remembered the stories she'd heard of people seeing a white light as they were dying. She seemed to catch a glimpse of something like that, but it was far away.

She moved her fingers in Jake's hand and felt him press against them in return. She wondered if she should have told Jake that she loved him. He'd never said the words to her, but suddenly it seemed important that he know.

The darkness overcame her, though, and she slipped into a sleep.

Chapter Thirteen

Jake willed himself not to panic. Cat had slipped into a peaceful sleep and he was able to feel the rhythm of her breathing from the pulse in the hand of hers he still held. Unfortunately, he should be working while she rested. He figured he'd have to go out on the streets of Miles City pretty soon and beg strangers to come in and give blood.

Just then he heard a hesitant footstep in the doorway and looked up.

"Mrs. Hargrove." He tried to keep his voice down so Cat wouldn't stir. "It sure is good to see you."

She might count as a friend. He'd always been nice to her, but now he needed to be charming.

The older woman stepped into the room with her gray hair clipped back with bobby pins and her metal cane in one hand. The other hand held a large shopping bag and she carried it over to the bed.

"Looking good today," he said with a thumbs-up gesture.

She looked startled by that. "Oh."

Then she nodded. "You've probably been up half the night."

He didn't know what to say to that so he kept quiet.

"Mary, out front, called and said you were looking for blood donors," Mrs. Hargrove said. "They never take mine anymore, but I put the word out before I left Dry Creek."

At first, Jake's heart leaped in triumph. Then he realized something. Those people had no reason to come. The ones who weren't clearing their fields to get them ready for plowing would be pressing their shirts for the wedding this afternoon. Anyone would rather go eat cake than drag themselves into Miles City and give blood. He'd never made himself popular in that town, either. "Tell them I'll pay every man, woman and child fifty dollars if they come here and give blood."

That should get him some action.

"You can't do that!" Mrs. Hargrove looked at him, truly aghast for the first time since he'd seen her today.

He might not be part of the community in Dry Creek, but Jake figured people there were pretty much like people everywhere.

He continued, "Make it a hundred for the first twenty people to come and show me their bandage. No cheating, though. I'll set up a system with the lab technician to check on everyone. I don't know what age a person needs to be to give blood, but teenagers are probably okay."

He would give away season tickets to the local football games if that's what it took.

"People need to be over one hundred and ten

pounds," Mrs. Hargrove said, her lips pinched together as though she didn't know what to do about him.

"Good, that will get the athletes," Jake said. "All that exercise should build good blood."

"But nobody pays for blood," she protested.

"I do," he said. "Today, I do."

Mrs. Hargrove looked at him for a minute or two, but she didn't say anything more. She might look a little disappointed in him, but he reasoned he was doing what he had to do. He couldn't afford to trust in some fairy tale that had people rushing around to do kind things for each other. Too much was at stake here. He'd buy his community of friends and worry about sentiment later.

There didn't seem much more to say and, finally, the woman reached in the bag she'd set on the bed and drew out a plant that stood about a foot tall. It wasn't much of a plant as far as Jake could see. Just a spindly green stalk growing up in a plain brown pot, the kind they gave away at the grocery stores.

"Your mom said Cat was interested in her lilac bushes, so I dug up a shoot from one of my bushes to give to her. Thought she might like it."

For some reason, Jake was able to look at that poor plant more easily than he could face Mrs. Hargrove, so he focused on it. "Hard to believe that thing blooms out with lilacs."

"God's creation is often that way."

Jake was grateful Mrs. Hargrove didn't have her flannel graph board with her. If she did, she'd compare him to a seed that fell on the side of the road and never grew. He'd heard the other kids talking about all the cut-out pictures she pressed onto the cloth in her Sunday-school class.

When she opened her mouth, he braced himself.

"Cat might want to plant some flowers of her own when this is all done," she said, instead of any of the words he thought she'd say. "I sit in my garden some days when I pray."

"She loves lilacs," Jake agreed, anxious to get off the subject of prayer and God. That was as bad as the flannel graph.

Mrs. Hargrove walked with the plant over to the windowsill. She set the plant down and placed an envelope beside it. "I brought a get-well card for her, too. It has a rose on it. They're my favorite and I figure anyone who likes lilacs is going to enjoy a rose."

"Why don't you open it up so she can see it from her bed," Jake suggested. Now that the danger of her talking to him about God had passed, he was grateful that she'd come.

The room was plain and didn't have any pictures, he suddenly noticed. It had an old television hanging in the corner, but that didn't add much to the decor. Maybe he should get someone to bring in a big poster with some flowers on it.

Mrs. Hargrove opened the envelope and slipped the card out. She carefully set it on the windowsill so Cat would see the pink rose on the front if she turned her head in bed.

"I brought a card for you, too." The woman walked back and pulled another card out of her bag. "I figure it's been too long since I sent you one."

Now, this was a surprise, he thought to himself as he took the card.

"Very nice," he said as he saw the landscape on the front. It looked like the Big Sheep Mountains in the back of the ranch. Then he opened it and saw the words she had scrawled. Her handwriting was a little harder to read than he remembered, but he knew the words even if half the letters were missing.

"Psalm 121, verses 1 and 2," he said, as he had a hundred times before.

"I didn't write out the words on this one," she apologized. "I have arthritis in my fingers these days."

"That's okay." He was ready for her. "'I will lift up mine eyes unto the hills, from whence cometh my help. My help cometh from the Lord, which made heaven and earth.'"

"You memorized it!"

Jake thought she couldn't have been more surprised if he had said it in Swahili.

"I didn't have much to do when I was in that home. It doesn't mean anything. I like to memorize." He didn't want her to think the Bible verses had been important to him, although he suspected they had been. All eleven of them.

She kept looking at him with that expectant expression on her face until he felt he had to say something more.

"God and I have never seen eye to eye," he finally explained. "I'm more the kind of guy who figures I better get it done on my own. So I kind of leave Him alone and He leaves me alone. But I..." He stopped.

Maybe he needed to just admit it. "I wish it were true that He cared. Even if I don't believe, I wish I could."

Mrs. Hargrove studied him hard for a moment, and then she began to smile. "You'll see. You just haven't needed Him enough to throw yourself at His feet yet. You can trust Him to help you believe."

There was no answer to that so he shrugged.

Regardless of how he felt about God, Jake did care about Mrs. Hargrove. When she was ready to leave, he walked her down to the parking lot, holding her elbow securely in his hand. "It's bad enough that my mother is having trouble walking, we don't need another person hobbling around for the wedding this afternoon."

"If you need someone to sit with Lara, just let me know," she said as they stood by her car.

"Oh, I hadn't thought," he muttered half to himself. "If all goes according to the schedule, they'll be doing Cat's surgery while the wedding is happening. I guess I never thought about where Lara would be. What do you think? She's only four."

Mrs. Hargrove nodded slowly. "That's right, but she'll grow up whether or not her mother makes it through this surgery. And I can't help but think she wouldn't want to remember that she'd been sent to a wedding instead of being as close as she could be to her mother."

Jake nodded. That made sense.

"I'll come and sit with her," Mrs. Hargrove offered as she opened the door on her car. "That way you can be with Cat before they take her into surgery and after she gets out. I'll bring some books for us, and Lara and I can sit quietly in one of the waiting rooms."

"She likes fairy tales." Jake held the door while Mrs. Hargrove slid into the driver's seat.

They said goodbye and he closed the door, turning to walk back to the hospital. He stopped at his pickup and got his hat that he'd left on the seat last night. Midway to the building, he stopped and looked at his watch. His money should have been wired to the places it needed to be and the airplane should have left Minneapolis by now. He should feel some satisfaction in a plan well executed, but he didn't. All he wanted was for Cat to live. He hurried back to her.

Cat lay in the hospital bed and she could feel her heart was stronger. Maybe it was because the doctor had just been in and said Jake had arranged everything for her surgery this afternoon. The man had a funny look on his face when he mentioned Jake, but she did not ask him why. She wondered instead how she could be falling in love more deeply when her heart might be winding down.

Maybe there was just clarity at the end, she thought as she rubbed her hand along the seams in the quilt that still covered her. As she'd struggled awake the last time, she'd started to wonder who had made the covering that lay on top of her. She had felt the age of the fabric and wondered if the quilt was older than Gracie. It had not been made by machine, she could tell that much by looking at the tiny stitches that so evenly connected the blocks of denim material.

Jake suddenly appeared in the doorway again and, at first, it seemed as though her imagination had conjured him up. He had his Stetson on his head now. His hands were cold when they touched her.

"Mrs. Hargrove left you a tiny lilac bush," he said as he pointed to the potted plant over on the windowsill. "And a card with a rose on it."

She watched his mouth move as he spoke to her. She was not making sense of all the words, but she loved to watch his mouth form the words.

"That's nice," she managed to say and closed her eyes. She would just rest a minute or two, she told herself. Then she remembered.

"Don't forget Lara," she said, her voice not as strong as it should be.

"I won't," Jake promised as he settled her hand under his again. "I talked to Wade and he's making arrangements to get her here. He said she needs to see you. She's worried."

Cat nodded. "She's such a sweet little girl."

"She's beautiful," Jake agreed softly, and she felt him smooth the hair back again and kiss her on the forehead.

"Wake me when she gets here," Cat whispered.

"I promise." Jake held her hand as she drifted into sleep.

She almost thought she felt someone kiss the back of her hand, but she couldn't force herself awake to find out. Nothing mattered, though. Not when Jake was guarding her.

Chapter Fourteen

Despite the dark clouds on the horizon, Jake knew it was close to noon by the way the sun still shone through the window. The surgeon should be landing in Billings in ten minutes. Everything was going according to plan, Jake assured himself. He had it under control.

Then he looked at Cat's pale face. She was sleeping and the doctor said that was good.

Nurses were rolling carts down the hall, delivering lunch trays, and one of them came into the room. She left a tray for Cat on the table at the foot of the bed. Then she looked at him and put down another tray. "Here you go, Mr. Goose."

"Huh?" He glanced up.

He wondered if he had missed some cartoon. He was having a hard time keeping track of all the people who had been in the room so far today, but he thought he'd remember if someone had turned the television on.

"That's what the staff decided to call you," the nurse explained. "You know how a goose will hang back with its mate if one of them is injured?"

He smiled even though his heart wasn't in it. "So they feed me for that?"

She nodded solemnly. "We respect geese here."

Jake looked down at where his hand was intertwined with Cat's. "There's nothing special about me. I've made lots of mistakes."

"But you're still here. That counts for something."

As the nurse was leaving, Wade came in holding a terra-cotta pot with a stake driven into its dirt.

"For Cat's garden," he said as he held it up. "A tomato plant. It's just starting. Amy got it from her aunt."

"Cat likes tomatoes," Jake said as he waved his hand at the windowsill. A half dozen other pots were already sitting there. The rumor that Cat wanted a garden had spread through Dry Creek almost faster than news that she needed blood for her surgery.

Wade held his arm up then and showed his bandage. "Amy will be up in a minute, she's giving blood now. And Mrs. Hargrove is bringing Lara in soon."

People had started showing up about an hour ago. Linda Enger from the Dry Creek Café was the first one, claiming she'd come as soon as she heard. She wore a hairnet and a white chef's apron wrapped around her waist, so Jake believed her. He hadn't seen her since he'd been sent to the home ten years ago, but that didn't seem to bother her. She came up and gave him a hug and left a pepper plant for Cat.

Two teenage boys, twins from the look of things, stood in the doorway next. They just flashed their wrists so he could see their bandages and then they left, shaking their heads, declining the fifty-dollar bills he'd pulled out of his wallet.

Then Elmer Maynard had shown up with another lilac bush, this one so tall Jake asked him to set it on the floor beneath the windowsill. The older man explained he couldn't give blood, but that he was making a donation to the Red Cross in Cat's name.

Then came Charley Nelson and his daughter-in-law Doris June Nelson, who was also Mrs. Hargrove's daughter.

They didn't want the fifty-dollar bills he'd waved around, either, and he wondered if he was offering too little. Maybe people expected him to pay later.

"I could write a check," he offered hesitantly to Doris June.

He remembered her and she'd always been pleasant to him. She was Mrs. Hargrove's daughter.

"Absolutely not," she told him firmly. Then she hugged him and welcomed him home.

He didn't know what to think. He liked to pay his way. At least he wouldn't feel so obligated to others then. The people of Dry Creek were chipping away at his resentment toward them. He was beginning to think that maybe they had done the best they could in his mother's trial. Maybe they didn't look down on his family as much as he had thought, either. They certainly seemed to be welcoming him home now.

Amy stood in the doorway then, her blond hair braided in some kind of a coronet on top of her head. Dainty pink flowers were worked into her hair in some mysterious way. She was wearing jeans and a cotton blouse, but her face was already starting to glow.

"You're going to be a beautiful bride," he told her as she flashed him her bandage. "I hope your dress has long sleeves."

"Nope," she said and grinned as she held her wrist high again. "But I wear the badge proudly."

"I have a crystal olive tray for you," he said to her then. "It's not wrapped yet, but I'll get it to you later."

She nodded, still in the doorway. "I love olives."

"So does Wade," he said. "So I predict a happy life together."

"Thanks," she said and rushed into the room to give him a tight hug.

"Don't cry," he whispered in her ear. "It's your wedding day. And all will be well."

She nodded at that and released him. A tear streaked down her cheek; then she turned and left.

Jake surprised himself by how sincere he had been when he told her that she'd have a good life with his brother. Maybe his mother was right about God giving a man another chance to be a better person. Wade was certainly doing better than Jake would have thought. If God could do that for his brother, maybe—

He heard a sound then and looked down at Cat. She turned slightly and blinked.

Her hair was matted against her head and she had dark circles under her eyes, but he could picture her as a bride as readily as he saw Amy in his mind.

Cat yawned and looked at him. He stroked her hand to help her wake up.

"Time?" she asked in a groggy voice.

He could see the clock if he looked through the door

and over to the nurse's station, so he craned his neck to find it. "Five minutes to twelve."

Then he saw two figures step into the doorway. Mrs. Hargrove and Lara were here.

"Pumpkin." Cat smiled and held out her arms.

Mrs. Hargrove let Lara go. The girl went running toward Cat and threw herself onto her bed.

"Hush, now," Cat said, putting her hand on Lara's little back. She could feel the sobs go clear through her daughter. Cat rubbed the girl's back for a minute or two. She could not afford tears of her own right now, but she had to soothe Lara.

"It's going to be all right," Cat whispered when her daughter's tears had slowed. "The doctor is coming to fix my heart so I can be with you for a long, long time."

Lara looked up at that, her tear-streaked face red from where she'd pressed it against Cat's chest.

"I have something important to tell you before I have surgery," Cat continued. She wasn't sure how long she could keep talking. "I'm sorry I haven't told you about your father sooner."

"I don't have a father," Lara said, her voice flat. "That's what the kids at preschool say."

"Well," Cat murmured. She hadn't known about that. "They only said that because they don't know. You do have a father."

She glanced over at Jake. His face was motionless. If she didn't know better, she would think he was scared. But nothing intimidated him. He bore the burdens of the world, but he wasn't worried about anything being more than he could handle.

Lara was listening intently.

"Is he a prince?" she asked hopefully. "I told the kids at school my father was a prince and he would take me to Disneyland because then I'd be his little princess."

"No, he's just a regular man," Cat said, even though there was probably nothing average about Jake. She suddenly wished she had written herself a script. How did one introduce a girl to her father? "But he—he's going to let you live with him if you can't live with Mommy for any reason."

Lara's eyes got big at that. She didn't say anything, but Cat believed she was beginning to understand.

"Are you going away?" her daughter whispered.

"Not because I want to." Cat forced her voice to stay strong. "And if I do, I want you to remember that I will love you always."

Lara nodded, but she wasn't moving.

Cat found she needed to stop talking for a moment. It was getting harder to breathe. She looked at Jake. "I can't tell her."

He nodded and cleared his throat. "What your mother wants you to know is that I'm your father."

Lara's mouth dropped open and she just stared at him.

Cat knew she should say something to reassure them both that they would come to love each other, that things would not be as difficult as they were both thinking at the moment, but the blackness was crowding close again. She closed her eyes to stop herself from passing out. She knew then more clearly than ever that her heart was in trouble. She could feel her body starting to gasp for life.

And then there was a bright flash of lightning that she could see even with her eyes closed. And moments later a clap to match.

"A thunderstorm," one of the nurses called out from the hallway.

She felt Jake's arm jerk as he stood up.

"Dear God, no," he prayed without realizing it.

She opened her eyes and saw him just standing there in the room. He glanced down at her and she understood his plans were not going well.

"It's all right." She moved her lips soundlessly.

He looked at her, stricken, but she could not focus any longer.

Jake was on the edge and felt as if he would fall. Then Mrs. Hargrove stepped into the room and grabbed his arm, anchoring him. "You don't know that the plane can't land yet. God is in control. He hears the prayers—"

"—of a righteous man," Jake finished for her. That had been another of the verses in his birthday cards.

"He also hears the prayers of a desperate man," she added.

Jake looked back at Cat. She was breathing; he could see her body strain to do so. He had never had to gamble on something so important before. Without her, his life would be nothing. But he was helpless. He had done everything he could to save her and it might not be enough. More money wasn't going to fix her heart. Sheer willpower wasn't the answer. He was out of tricks and maneuvers.

Cat opened her eyes again and smiled at him.

Then he followed her gaze over to where Lara sat on the edge of the bed. He needed to do something for all of them. He might not be the prince Lara wanted, but he was all she had. He walked around the bed and picked her up in his arms. He did not know how they were going to manage, but he was going to be her father.

He put his hand on her back to steady her as he stood there.

Cat's eyes fluttered as she looked at the two of them together and the alarms on the machines started to go off again. Jake stepped back this time and let Lara press her face into his chest for comfort.

The nurses came in and this time it did not take long to get Cat stabilized.

The doctor entered the room just as they were leaving.

"I got a call that the plane landed early. The surgeon's almost here." He turned to the nurses. "Let's get her prepped and to the operating room."

Jake watched them wheel Cat out of the room. It felt as though they were taking his heart with them.

He looked around and saw Mrs. Hargrove just outside the door. She was standing against the wall opposite Cat's room and she had her head bent in prayer. She seemed to know that he needed her, though, because she raised her head and came into the room.

"I need to go with Cat," he said as he looked down at his daughter.

Mrs. Hargrove nodded. "I'll take Lara to the waiting room."

"Thanks. I'll be along there soon. They won't let me

stay for the surgery, but I want to be there as long as I can."

He looked at Lara then and tried to smile.

"I'm glad you're my daughter," he whispered to her as he set her down so she could walk over to Mrs. Hargrove.

"Pray for me," he told Mrs. Hargrove as she held out her hand to Lara.

The woman looked up and nodded as though she had expected him to say something like that.

"God has had you in His sights for some time now," she said. "You just need to trust Him with everything you have."

Those words pounded through Jake's mind as he ran down the hallway after the team taking Cat to the operating room. Everything he had was her. He caught her before they wheeled her into the room.

He needed to trust God for her and their future.

"I love you, Cat Barker," he leaned down and said. Her eyes were closed, but he saw the smile on her face. "And I'm going to turn my life around. No more gambling. If God can make a new man out of my brother, he can make a new man out of me."

"I love you, too," she whispered and opened her eyes.

The wheels of the gurney had started up again, but he walked alongside her.

"You're going to have to marry me," he said.

"We'll have a lilac wedding," she agreed.

The gurney came to a doorway and stopped.

Jake bent down and brushed his lips across hers. "I'm going to move home to Dry Creek and build a house for us there—you, me and Lara. Wade wants me to be his partner on the ranch. If that's what you want. If not, we can live anywhere, do anything. As long as we're together."

"Dry Creek is our home," she whispered. "That's where we belong."

Just then one of the nurses cleared her throat and turned to Jake. "I'm afraid you'll have to go to the waiting room."

Jake nodded. "I'll be there with Lara."

"Love her for me," Cat said, her voice so weak he could barely hear.

"Always," he vowed as the nurses pushed the gurney into the operating room and the door closed behind them.

Jake stood there for a moment before he forced himself to walk back to the waiting room. The hall was longer than he remembered, but he still hadn't figured out what to say to Lara by the time he was at the doorway.

Someone had partially closed the curtains and the light in the room was subdued. Mrs. Hargrove was sitting on a chair and Lara was curled up on the older woman's lap.

"I—" Jake began.

Lara turned to look up at him and he saw from the worry on her face that there was no need for words. His daughter slid down to the floor and ran to him. He bent down and picked her up, holding her close.

"It's going to be okay," he whispered as he carried her back into the room.

Mrs. Hargrove patted a chair next to her and he sat down, with Lara cuddled in his arms.

Jake realized his daughter was crying and he panicked for a moment, wondering if he'd know what to do, but then he started rubbing her back and he felt her breathing even out. They sat there together, like that, until Lara finally fell asleep.

Even then, Jake did not move. Mrs. Hargrove left to make some telephone calls and, when she returned, she had a piece of paper with her.

"I called the prayer chain at church to let them know the surgery was happening now," the older woman whispered as she sat back down. "Some of the folks wanted me to pass on their greetings to you. I wrote them down so I wouldn't forget what everyone said."

"Me?" He was surprised. "I've been gone from Dry Creek for so long."

"You're still one of us," Mrs. Hargrove said as she put the paper in his left hand. His right arm was supporting Lara. "You can read everything later. They just want you to know they're praying."

"I'm—" Jake began, but had to swallow "—grateful. Very, very grateful."

He'd never needed people before, and he was humbled that his old neighbors would pray for the woman he loved. What was left of the bitterness in his heart crumbled. He had no defenses against that kind of care. The people in Dry Creek were going to be his friends again and he felt very fortunate to have them.

Jake sat with Lara in his arms for what seemed like hours. No one except Mrs. Hargrove came into the room. He wondered if the hospital had another waiting area or if there was just no one else who needed to be there.

When it seemed he couldn't wait any longer, a man in green scrubs came through the doorway. Jake knew he was the surgeon even though this was his first glimpse of the man.

"She's going to be fine," the surgeon said and grinned widely. "Everything went perfectly. She should have a healthy, full life from now on."

"When can I see her?" Jake asked. He started to stand, forgetting he held Lara. The movement caused her to stir in his arms and he sat back down.

"Mommy?" his daughter asked.

"She's going to be fine," he whispered.

"I'll have someone come get you when Miss Barker is out of the recovery room," the surgeon said as he turned and walked back to the door. "It won't be long. One visitor at a time."

Jake just sat there when the surgeon left. He hadn't realized how stressed he had been until he felt the relief rush through him.

"She's going to be okay." He turned to Mrs. Hargrove and said the words for the pure pleasure of hearing them himself.

The older woman nodded, blinking back tears. "I'll sit with Lara while you go see her and then I'll call everyone and let them know the surgery is over and all is well. It'll take Cat a while before she's able to talk and I'm sure she'll want Lara to see her when she's more herself."

Jake nodded and then it hit him. Now that Cat was going to live, she might not still want to marry him. It was one thing for a woman to agree to a man's proposal when she was facing surgery. But now that she had her whole life ahead of her, she might have other plans.

By the time the nurse came to take him to Cat, Jake was not breathing easily. But the minute he entered the darkened room where Cat lay, he knew only one thing was important. His beloved Cat was alive.

"Don't worry about anything," he whispered as he bent down to kiss her cheek. He was talking to himself as much as Cat. Her eyes were still closed and her skin was cool where his lips touched it.

"It'll be a few more minutes before she can answer," the nurse said to him as she checked the machines attached to Cat.

"I'll wait," Jake said as he reached behind himself and pulled a chair close to the bed. Then he sat down and reached for Cat's hand, threading his fingers through hers. "I'm just so happy."

The nurse left then, and Jake sat there watching Cat breathe.

Finally, she turned her head toward him and opened her eyes. "Jake?"

She seemed surprised to see him and he wondered if she was. He had not been there when she needed him too many times already.

"I'm never going to leave you again," he said softly. And then he wondered if he was presuming too much. "If you don't want me to, that is…"

He looked down and her eyes were smiling at him. "I'll always want you with me."

Jake blinked back his tears. "Then I'll be there."
"Promise?" Cat whispered.
He nodded. "With my whole heart."
Then he bent to kiss her again.

Epilogue

Two months later

Cat took a deep breath, savoring the fragrance of the lilac bushes. Max had come up early from Las Vegas and had helped Jake build an arch yesterday where the old clothesline had stood so she would have something to walk under when Doris June played the wedding march on her keyboard today. The lilacs were in full bloom elsewhere around Dry Creek and people had been donating branches all morning so that huge lilac bouquets stood beside the folding chairs on the lawn in front of Gracie's bushes.

Cat had her wedding dress on and had snuck out of the house to be sure everything was ready for the guests that would be arriving soon.

"Mommy." Lara came running up to her from the back door of the Stone house. She was wearing a frilly, little white dress with lilac-colored trim. She was holding a square package wrapped in silver paper and a larger one in red. "I have presents and it's not even my birthday!"

"I see that," Cat said as she looked up to see Jake following their daughter out of the house, carrying yet another wrapped box, this one in ivory paper.

"More presents?" she asked when he came closer. She put her hand up to straighten his tie. He was wearing his wedding suit and was more handsome than any man had a right to be. He kept the box in his hands, though, instead of giving it to Lara.

He shrugged. "I'm only responsible for the small one. The big red box is from my mother and she won't even tell me what's in it."

"It's my princess gift," Lara announced.

"Oh." Cat frowned as she leaned down as much as she could in the full skirt. White lace nestled in with the green grass. "We talked about that, remember? You have a mommy and a daddy now—a real one. You don't need to be a princess any longer."

Lara stood there, mutiny in her eyes.

"Jake?" Cat looked up.

"I'm afraid my mother did call it her princess gift," he admitted.

"Well, I guess it is a special day for all of us," Cat conceded as she stood up. "So go ahead and open them."

Cat was surprised when her daughter reached for the silver gift first.

"It's from my daddy," she whispered as though that explained everything. And maybe it did. Lara and Jake were inseparable these days.

"Ohhh," Lara sighed when she pulled out a string of iridescent white pearls. "They're pretty."

"I thought they'd go with your dress," Jake said, not quite suppressing his smile at Lara's delight.

Lara lifted up the necklace to her mother. "Put it on me."

"The pearls are very nice," Cat said to Jake as she clasped the necklace around her daughter's neck.

"And this one's for you," Jake said as he handed her the box wrapped in ivory paper.

"What is it?" Lara asked, her excitement apparent.

Cat slipped the paper off and then the lid of the box. "Oh, my! The goblets we saw. Oh, Jake, you went back in and bought them."

He shook his head. "No, I bought them the day we saw them. I think even then I was hoping we could use them when we cut our cake."

"They're so lovely," she said, blinking back tears. Then she turned, intending to kiss Jake.

But she was distracted by a rustling at her feet before she could meet his lips, and they both looked down. Lara was ripping the paper off the red box.

"Take it easy," Cat said even though she had no hopes of slowing her daughter down.

Finally, the box was bare of wrapping and Lara stopped.

It was silent for a bit.

"What do you think it is?" their daughter asked, turning to Cat and Jake.

Cat felt her heart twist to see that her daughter was still uncertain about what lay ahead in her life. Hopefully, the years to come in Dry Creek would make her more secure. They had all joined the church here and were growing closer to God. In time, her daughter would be confident, but now she clearly wasn't.

"We don't know, sweetheart," Jake said softly. "You'll have to open it to find out."

Lara slowly lifted the lid off the box and then gave a cry of joy as she pulled out what looked to Cat like a bunch of feathers. There were gray ones, white ones, and a few that had a beautiful lilac tinge to them. Then she saw a leather band with shiny lilac beads around it and saw that the rows of feathers were attached.

"It's a chief's headdress," Jake finally said as he began to chuckle. "My mother's reminding us that Lara is a princess, after all, because her great-great-something-grandfather was a big chief of the Cherokee. That makes her a real Indian princess."

By now, Lara had put the headdress on and was looking around in delight.

Cat started to smile, too. "That is the best kind of princess to be."

And then she looked up at the man who was going to be her husband. "And I guess that makes you a prince."

He grinned at that. "A prince who—with God's help—is going to do his best to see that we all live happily ever after."

With that, he bent down to kiss her.

Cat couldn't help but notice that her daughter nodded in approval.

* * * * *

Dear Reader,

It's spring again and, if you're like me, that signals a time for new hope. Something stirs in each of us when we see new green shoots of grass or plants come to life after a hard winter. On the family farm where I grew up in Montana, my mother had lilac bushes and, if my sisters and I left our bedroom window open at night, we went to sleep with the fragrance of the bushes all around us. Maybe that's why spring, in my mind, always smells like lilacs.

I'm sure you have similar memories and I hope this book will remind you that new beginnings are still possible—whether it's in a relationship or some other place that is broken in your life. Remember all things are possible with God's help.

If you have a minute, I'd love to hear from you. Just contact me through my website at www.janettronstad.com. In the meantime, God bless you and keep you.

Sincerely,

Janet Tronstad

Questions for Discussion

1. What character did you most identify with in the book? Who and why?

2. Jake Stone longs for home and, at the same time, doesn't want to go home. Is there something in your life that you long for and believe you will never see again, or find in the first place? If so, what words from God come to mind when you think of it?

3. Jake believes the fact that his father was an abusive man taints his own ability to be a good parent. Our parents influence us profoundly. In what ways have you parents influenced you?

4. Jake and his brothers couldn't think of any words for their father's tombstone. If you could write something for them, what would it be?

5. Jake's mother lied to protect her sons from suspicion in the murder of her husband. Was she right to lie? How did it complicate things?

6. When his mother was sent to prison, Jake's life abruptly changed. Who did he blame for the change in everything? If you were in his situation, who would you blame?

7. Jake couldn't bring himself to write to his mother when she was in prison. Is there someone you wish

you could write a letter, but can't because you don't know what to say? How would you counsel Jake if you could talk to him?

8. Jake had delayed going home when his mother got out of prison because he felt awkward for not writing. Have you ever delayed doing something because you felt like that?

9. Even though Jake sent his old friend, Cat Barker, money, he didn't write to her. How would you interpret this if you were in her shoes? What did it really mean?

10. Cat Barker needed surgery and she was worried about what would happen to her daughter if she died. The chaplain at the hospital had been able to guide her back to God, but she still worried. Does God take away all our worry? Should He?

INSPIRATIONAL

Love Inspired.

celebrating
15
YEARS

COMING NEXT MONTH
AVAILABLE MARCH 27, 2012

HER LONE STAR COWBOY
Mule Hollow Homecoming
Debra Clopton

A LOVE REKINDLED
A Town Called Hope
Margaret Daley

SWEETHEART REUNION
Lenora Worth

REDEMPTION RANCH
Leann Harris

HER FAMILY WISH
Betsy St. Amant

LOVE OF A LIFETIME
Carol Voss

REQUEST YOUR FREE BOOKS!

2 FREE INSPIRATIONAL NOVELS
PLUS 2
FREE
MYSTERY GIFTS

Love Inspired.

YES! Please send me 2 FREE Love Inspired® novels and my 2 FREE mystery gifts (gifts are worth about $10). After receiving them, if I don't wish to receive any more books, I can return the shipping statement marked "cancel." If I don't cancel, I will receive 6 brand-new novels every month and be billed just $4.49 per book in the U.S. or $4.99 per book in Canada. That's a saving of at least 22% off the cover price. It's quite a bargain! Shipping and handling is just 50¢ per book in the U.S. and 75¢ per book in Canada.* I understand that accepting the 2 free books and gifts places me under no obligation to buy anything. I can always return a shipment and cancel at any time. Even if I never buy another book, the two free books and gifts are mine to keep forever.

105/305 IDN FEGR

Name	(PLEASE PRINT)

Address	Apt. #

City	State/Prov.	Zip/Postal Code

Signature (if under 18, a parent or guardian must sign)

Mail to the **Reader Service:**
IN U.S.A.: P.O. Box 1867, Buffalo, NY 14240-1867
IN CANADA: P.O. Box 609, Fort Erie, Ontario L2A 5X3

Not valid for current subscribers to Love Inspired books.

**Are you a subscriber to Love Inspired books
and want to receive the larger-print edition?
Call 1-800-873-8635 or visit www.ReaderService.com.**

* Terms and prices subject to change without notice. Prices do not include applicable taxes. Sales tax applicable in N.Y. Canadian residents will be charged applicable taxes. Offer not valid in Quebec. This offer is limited to one order per household. All orders subject to credit approval. Credit or debit balances in a customer's account(s) may be offset by any other outstanding balance owed by or to the customer. Please allow 4 to 6 weeks for delivery. Offer available while quantities last.

Your Privacy—The Reader Service is committed to protecting your privacy. Our Privacy Policy is available online at www.ReaderService.com or upon request from the Reader Service.

We make a portion of our mailing list available to reputable third parties that offer products we believe may interest you. If you prefer that we not exchange your name with third parties, or if you wish to clarify or modify your communication preferences, please visit us at www.ReaderService.com/consumerschoice or write to us at Reader Service Preference Service, P.O. Box 9062, Buffalo, NY 14269. Include your complete name and address.

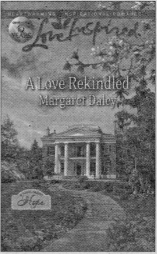

For a sneak peek of Shirlee McCoy's heart-stopping inspirational romantic suspense UNDERCOVER BODYGUARD, read on!

"It's okay," Ryder said, pulling Shelby into his arms.

But it wasn't okay, and they both knew it.

A woman was dead, and there was nothing either of them could do to change it.

"How can it be when Maureen is dead?" Shelby asked, looking up into his face as if he might have some way to fix things. He didn't, and he'd stopped believing in his own power and invincibility long ago.

"It will be. Eventually. Come on. You need to get the bump on your head looked at."

"I don't have time for that. I have to get back to the bakery. It's Friday. The busiest day of the week." Her teeth chattered on the last word, her body trembling. He draped his coat around her shoulders.

"Better?" he asked, and she nodded.

"I can't seem to stop shaking. I mean, one minute, I'm preparing to deliver pastries to my friend and the next she's gone. I just can't believe….." Her voice trailed off, her eyes widening as she caught sight of his gun holster.

"You've got a gun."

"Yes."

"Are you a police officer?"

"Security contractor."

"You're a bodyguard?"

"I'm a security contractor. I secure people and things."

"A bodyguard," she repeated, and he didn't argue.

Two fire trucks and an ambulance lined the curb in front of the house, and firefighters had already hooked a hose to the hydrant. Water streamed over the flames but did little to douse the fire.

Suddenly, an EMT ran toward them. "Is she okay?"

"She was knocked unconscious by the force of the explosion. She has a bad gash on her head."

"Let me take a look." The EMT edged him out of the way, and Ryder knew it was time to go talk to the fire marshal and the police officers who'd just arrived, and let the EMT take Shelby to the hospital.

But she grabbed his hand before he moved away, her grip surprisingly strong. "Are you leaving?"

"Do you want me to, Shelby Ann?" he asked.

"You can leave."

"I know that I can, but do you *want* me to?"

"I…haven't decided, yet."

Pick up UNDERCOVER BODYGUARD for the rest of Shelby and Ryder's exciting, suspenseful love story, available in April 2012, only from Love Inspired® Books Love Inspired® Suspense.